BUNKER
10

BUNKER 10

J.A. HENDERSON

OXFORD
UNIVERSITY PRESS

OXFORD
UNIVERSITY PRESS

Great Clarendon Street, Oxford OX2 6DP

Oxford University Press is a department of the University of Oxford.
It furthers the University's objective of excellence in research, scholarship,
and education by publishing worldwide in

Oxford New York

Auckland Cape Town Dar es Salaam Hong Kong Karachi
Kuala Lumpur Madrid Melbourne Mexico City Nairobi
New Delhi Shanghai Taipei Toronto

With offices in

Argentina Austria Brazil Chile Czech Republic France Greece
Guatemala Hungary Italy Japan Poland Portugal Singapore
South Korea Switzerland Thailand Turkey Ukraine Vietnam

Oxford is a registered trade mark of Oxford University Press
in the UK and in certain other countries

British Library Cataloguing in Publication Data

Data available

ISBN-13: 978-0-19-275486-8

3 5 7 9 10 8 6 4 2

Typeset by Newgen Imaging Systems (P) Ltd., Chennai, India
Printed in Great Britain by
Cox & Wyman Ltd, Reading, Berkshire

Thanks to Charlotte, Emily, Jodi, Katherine, Mandy, Mo, PsychoCat, Siobhan, and Sarah for their invaluable help (e.g. saying things like 'that doesn't make any sense' and 'I don't think you spell Leutanant that way')

For Willie Schmidt

When I do television interviews about time travel, the first question I am always asked is this: 'What if you went back in time and killed your grandmother before she gave birth to your mother?' The problem is obvious: if you kill your grandmother, then your mother would have never been born, and you would never have been born; if you were never born, you could never go back in time, and so you could not kill your grandmother. This conundrum, known as the Grandmother Paradox, is often thought sufficiently potent to rule out time travel to the past.

J. Richard Gott

PINEGROVE MILITARY INSTALLATION

Monday 24 December 2007

20.00 hours

The Christmas tree was taller than a military cadet and just as green. It had been decorated with old-fashioned wooden ornaments, wrapped in thick tinsel strands, and dotted with real candles in silver holders.

Seven children sat on the dormitory floor in a ring, ignoring the thin line of smoke seeping under the door. Simon and May-Rose pulled crackers. Barn, Cruikshank, and Diddy Dave swapped presents. Lesley and Jimmy Hicks had their arms round each other, paper hats upon their heads, pretending to be the King and Queen of Christmas.

'We've run out of Coca-Cola.' Barn thumped his chest. 'I need more Coke if I'm going to do the biggest burp in world history. And I really am,' he added proudly.

'You're gonnae throw up, ya big balloon.' Diddy Dave draped a clump of discarded ribbons over his friend's head.

'I'll get the drinks.' Simon pulled himself up, went to the door and opened it.

The corridor outside was filled with oily smoke, thickest where it rolled across the ceiling in black folds, a churning, suffocating beast. Two dead soldiers in British army uniform lay on the ground, staring sightlessly at each other. Simon put a handkerchief over his mouth, stepped over the bloody corpses, and went to the canteen. He fetched a bottle of Coke from one of the tall grey fridges and returned to the party. Shutting the door behind him, he handed the bottle to Barn who took a huge swig and grinned at the others.

'Ready?'

Simon looked at his watch and shook his head. 'It's eight o'clock,' he said sadly.

Jimmy Hicks pulled Lesley close and held her tight. Barn began praying. May-Rose started to cry. Simon screwed his eyes shut and put his hands over his ears.

A high-pitched sound, louder than the whistle of a steam train, rose from below and vast white light, bright as the promise of life, enveloped the room and ripped it apart.

At twenty hundred hours on Monday, 24th December 2007, Pinegrove Military Installation exploded.

The blast ripped apart acres of forest and devastated the remote highland valley where the base was located. There were no survivors and no official cause was given for the incident.

Inside Pinegrove were a hundred and eighty-five male and female military personnel—a mixture of scientists and soldiers.

There were also seven children.

This is the story of their last day.

PART I

PINEGROVE MILITARY INSTALLATION

Monday 24 December 2007

08.00 hours—13.00 hours

08.00

Jimmy Hicks wondered if the army would consider shooting a fifteen year old. After all, what he intended to do amounted to treason.

Hicks sauntered through Pinegrove's complex of corridors, dressed in jeans and a sweatshirt, a satchel over one shoulder and a book in his hand. He was a tall slim boy, so he slouched to compensate and it made his wavy brown hair flop over his forehead. If it hadn't been for the fact that he was in a military facility, he would have looked like any ordinary schoolboy on his way to class. Even the colour of the passageways looked right—a dull industrial beige that adorned so many school hall-ways.

Jimmy read as he walked. Or he pretended to read, but his eyes kept darting upwards, scanning the ceiling.

There were small security cameras set at regular intervals into the roof—and those were just the ones he could see. That was good, though. It meant there were too many screens for the staff in the Operations Room to monitor properly. As long as the boy didn't do anything obvious he wouldn't attract attention.

He passed the living quarters and carried on down the corridor. An armed guard at the end of the passage gave a friendly nod and pointed to the book.

'It's Christmas Eve, Jimmy. No lessons today.'

The guard had no doubt Jimmy Hicks knew this. After all, the boy was a genius.

'Just walking and reading, Bill. That way I get physical exercise along with my mental stimulation.'

'Oh. Right.' The guard glanced at the book cover. *Cosmology in Gauge Field Theory and String Theory* by D. Bailin.

'What the hell are you reading?'

'The physics lab was out of comic books.'

'When I was your age *I* had my head stuck in a *Beano*,' Bill laughed. His smile faded as he realized how dumb *that* must sound—Jimmy Hicks had a security clearance higher than his own. The boy stuffed the book into his bag.

'Yeah. Maybe I should get out more.'

'One weekend leave a month, son, same as me.'

'But *I* get escorted to Glen Isla village at the weekend—there's nothing but a post office and a couple of farmhouses. You do what you like with *your* time off.'

'It's Christmas Eve and I'm here, aren't I?' the guard retorted. 'I'm in the army, Jimmy. I don't have the luxury of doing what I want.'

Jimmy Hicks couldn't argue with that. He pushed his hands in his pockets and leaned against the wall.

'How come all Christmas leave is cancelled, Bill?' he asked nonchalantly. 'Nobody tells me anything in this place.'

The guard had a lumpy red face and a bulbous nose. Put a white beard on him, Jimmy thought, and he'd make a passable Saint Nicholas.

'Nice try, son.' Bill looked around at the empty passageway, then relaxed and let his shoulders sag. 'All I know is that something big has come up and now we're all stuck here. At this time of year we're operating on a skeleton crew as it is. There's nobody spare to escort you and the other kids home.'

His jowls drooped a little more and he smacked his lips in disapproval.

'I'm sorry you can't spend Christmas with your folks.'

'If you ever met my parents you wouldn't say that.' Jimmy Hicks fished a bag of half-melted toffees out of his pocket. 'Like a sweet?'

The paper was dark with stains and crusted with brown globs. Bill wrinkled his nose and shook his head.

'I must have been standing too near a radiator.' Jimmy dropped the gooey mess into a stainless-steel bin next to the door. It hit the bottom with a loud thunk—the bin had been emptied half an hour earlier.

But Jimmy Hicks already knew that.

Inside the sweet bag, nestled among the sticky lumps of toffee, was a small transmitter, no larger than a finger.

He had now planted six transmitters between this point and the workstation in his dormitory—all hidden in waste receptacles. He had designed the devices himself to work as a relay booster system. Now, if he sent a wireless transmission from his computer in the dorm, each hidden device would amplify that signal before sending it on to the next. By the time his transmission reached the last tiny booster it would have enough power to pull a 747 out of the sky.

The bins would be emptied again at 07.00 tomorrow morning. The rubbish would be compacted and all evidence of the transmitters would be obliterated. By that time, however, they would have done their job and he would be gone.

Jimmy shouldered his bag and raised his hand.

'Merry Christmas, Bill.'

'See you tomorrow, pal.' The guard pulled his droopy face into what he hoped was a festive grin. Jimmy waved briefly and strolled back the way he had come. A small smile twitched on the corners of his lips and he turned his face away from the cameras, letting his floppy hair hide the mischievous twinkle in his eyes.

Since it contained living areas, level one of Pinegrove military base was a low security area—until you reached the far end. There the passageway became a high security zone, hence the guard. Pinegrove's Operations Room was at the end of the corridor and Jimmy certainly didn't have clearance to go *there*.

Never mind. The last transmitter was close enough.

So far Jimmy Hicks knew he hadn't done anything seriously wrong. If the devices were discovered and traced to him, he'd say it was part of a private experiment he was conducting. Top Brass wouldn't believe him, of course—he'd be labelled a security risk and expelled from his studies at Pinegrove.

But at least he wouldn't be shot.

Once he activated the boosters, however, Jimmy would be crossing a line. He'd be interfering with the security of a top secret UK government facility. He'd be sabotaging a supposedly foolproof defence system. Most of all, he'd be pitting his wits against some of the finest and most ruthless military minds in the world.

His heart was pounding but he gave a grim smile.

The challenge was partly why he was doing this.

But, if he *were* caught, the powers that be would never believe his other reason.

He wanted to impress a girl.

09.20

In the cab of the drab, olive truck Lieutenant Dunwoody opened his sealed orders. The vehicle headed a small convoy heading north and the lieutenant held the envelope between his knees while he removed the contents.

Inside were a few photographs and a thin file marked **TOP SECRET**. Dunwoody studied them carefully, memorizing the contents.

There was an aerial view of Pinegrove—the military installation he was heading for—surrounded by thick forest and ringed by a double perimeter fence. It didn't look much, just a handful of box-shaped, fortified buildings. According to an attached report, however, this was because most of the base was underground.

Dunwoody glanced at the driver but the soldier was concentrating on traversing a winding highland road not much wider than his truck. The lieutenant bent over the report again.

Officially Pinegrove specialized in virtual technology and, to some extent, this was true. The facility boasted the most advanced reality simulators in the world—designed to put soldiers into combat scenarios and test their reactions. Plugged into one of Pinegrove's virtual settings, an officer might find himself facing hostile tribesmen in the

Somalian desert. He could be trapped in a war-ravaged Middle-Eastern street by an armed mob. He might be ordered to evacuate civilians from a burning village under heavy mortar fire.

According to *this* classified report, however, Pinegrove researched more than virtual technology.

Under the base was a labyrinth of laboratories and associated living quarters, six levels in all. Teams at the installation worked on projects as diverse as skin grafting technology, three dimensional mapping, and alternative fuel cells. Above ground, all that could be seen were the Administration Offices, the Vehicle Maintenance Depot, and a building known as the West Wing.

The West Wing consisted of staff training areas and two specially adapted dormitories.

For some reason these dormitories contained children, but the report didn't say why.

Dunwoody mentally filed this unusual information, though it didn't concern him much. The kind of squad he commanded wasn't sent out to deal with trivia.

He and his men had been ordered to Pinegrove because of a problem in the lower levels—an area so highly classified that the report didn't say *what* they would find down there.

And *that* concerned Lieutenant Dunwoody a great deal.

10.00

Jimmy Hicks was thinking.

He sat in a straight-backed chair, in the centre of the dormitory, staring at the wall. Every now and then he twisted a strand of hair round his finger and pulled at it, as if he were coaxing an idea from his head. The other kids ignored him, used to his spells of intense concentration. If it turned out he was having an extraordinary notion then, sooner or later, he'd go next door for peace and quiet. If the idea wasn't going anywhere then neither would he, and he'd eventually join in the conversation.

This particular exchange was about the possibility of time travel. The children in the dormitory were all geniuses. They didn't talk about mundane topics.

'If ah managed tae build a time machine, ah'd use it tae bet on the horses, know?' Diddy Dave laced thin white hands behind his head, pushing a Burberry baseball cap over his beady eyes. He was a pale, sharp-faced fourteen year old, dressed permanently in a shell suit and white trainers. 'I'd take the winnings, play the stock market. Afore ye know it, ahm minted. Next stop, a wee island in the Pacific for me; a semi-detached in the suburbs for mah maw.'

'Time travel doesn't work that way.' Simon sniffed, looking up from the formula he was scribbling in a plastic notepad. 'Even something as

14

trivial as attending a horse race could have serious repercussions in the future.'

'Dinnae get carried away, man. Ah'd go tae the bookies in Spam Valley, where naebody would rat me oot, know?'

'I've no idea what you just said.'

At thirteen Simon was the youngest of the boys—quiet and a little shy, with unruly hair and round glasses.

'Listen, Harry Potter,' Dave pointed a menacing finger at his bespectacled companion, 'ye dinnae grow up on a Glasgow housing estate soundin' like you've got a mooth full o' marbles, know?' He glanced around scornfully at his companions. 'You wi' yer nose aye stuck in a book and Hicksy, wi' his girly hair? Ye wouldne last five minutes where I grew up without getting a smack in the gob.'

He glanced across at Barn who was lying on the floor reading a comic.

'Well, maybe the big man could.'

Dave had a point—Barn's size was truly impressive for a fourteen year old.

'I saw a TV show about Glasgow once.' Barn propped himself up on a fleshy arm and looked lazily at his companions. 'I think it was *Crimewatch*.'

Simon gave a snigger. Barn was a mathematical genius and could calculate incredibly complex equations in his head. But in every other way he was slower than normal children. Often it was hard to tell when he was joking.

'Aye, well maybe.' Dave looked proudly down at his gleaming clothes. 'Ye dinnae get togs like these without a bit of nickin', eh? Ahm wearin' mair labels than a jam factory, man.'

'You wrap your presents in Burberry paper, don't you?' Simon grunted.

'Two layers, man.'

'We won't be getting any presents this year, will we?' Barn said unhappily. 'This doesn't seem much like Christmas.'

'What you bumpin' yer gums aboot, big man?' Dave pointed over his shoulder. 'We've got a tree, eh?'

In the corner of the room was an unsteady looking pine sapling. One of the base soldiers had pulled it out of the forest and dragged it upstairs to the dormitory when he found out the children weren't going home for the holidays. Now it sat in a cleaning bucket which was too small for its weight, and the children kept it upright by leaning it against a filing cabinet. To try and cheer up the bedraggled plant, Simon had hung test tubes filled with coloured liquid from its branches. Unfortunately he only had three to spare.

'We've got to decorate this thing properly and get a bigger pot,' he grunted.

'You think I should put up a stocking?' Barn asked solemnly. 'I always got a sock filled with oranges on Christmas day.'

'You sure it wasnae a sack filled with chocolate oranges?' Dave smirked.

'Sorry, Barn,' Simon said regretfully. 'If Santa tried to come down a chimney here, they'd shoot him for trespassing on government property.'

The large boy went back to reading his comic, but his bottom lip was trembling.

'Now look what ye've done, ya bam. Barn's in a total huff.'

Simon hunkered down beside the large boy.

'Listen,' he said confidentially, 'I've been working on a special Christmas present and you'll see it tomorrow. You're going to love it. Everyone is.'

'I dinnae want some toilet roll cover that you crocheted yersel'.' Diddy Dave launched his cap at Simon who swatted it away. It whizzed past Jimmy Hicks and the boy looked round, startled.

'Whit ye thinking there, Hicksy?' Dave called. 'Yiv no' said nothing for an hour.'

Barn and Simon looked expectant. All of the children in the dormitory had phenomenal mental skills of some sort or other, but Jimmy Hicks's IQ was off the scale. It was possible that, some day, one of his ideas would change the world.

'I was wondering what to wear tonight.'

'Eh?'

'I want to look good.' Jimmy Hicks nodded solemnly to himself. 'I'm going on a date.'

'Ye dancer! You chasin' booty, man?'

'Is it Lesley from next door?' Simon asked.

Jimmy Hicks nodded again. 'I think she likes me in black.'

Barn sat up and looked around, bright blue eyes narrowing in his heavy face. The dormitory was clean and antiseptic. Rows of neatly made beds, each with an adjoining locker, lined the walls. Steel mesh latticed the tinted glass in the windows.

Simon guessed what was puzzling the larger boy.

'With all those fashion problems on your mind, Jimmy,' he pointed out, 'you probably just forgot we're inside a top secret base.'

'Aye. Where ye gonnae take her?' Dave jeered. 'The canteen?'

'I thought a moonlight stroll through the forest and then watch the sun rise over the mountains.'

'That sounds romantic,' Simon agreed. 'All you have to do is get past the armed guards, closed circuit cameras topped with lasers, and double barbed-wire fence.'

'Aye, Romeo. Then figure oot how tae get back in, know?'

Jimmy Hicks smiled and his eyes sparkled with dark intelligence.

'I already have.'

There was a snort of derision from the corner.

Cruikshank—the last of the boys in the room— rolled over in his bunk and raised a disbelieving eyebrow. He was a handsome boy with platinum blond hair and bright green eyes. He *could* be friendly and charming when he wanted. He just didn't want to very often.

'How do you propose to get in and out of the base undetected?' he said casually. The others nodded in unison, intrigued as to how their friend intended to pull off this near-impossible feat.

'I'll need everyone's help, of course.' Jimmy Hicks smiled.

'Oh aye?' Dave grunted. 'An' whit's in it fur us?'

'You got anything *more* interesting to do on

Christmas Eve?' Jimmy nodded at the bare dormitory. 'If we pull this off we'll be able to sneak off the base *whenever* we want. No more monthly jaunts to some tiny village in the middle of nowhere.'

Barn gave a loud yawn. 'I like the countryside.'

'That's because you look like a farm animal.'

'I like any outside,' Barn replied, nonplussed. 'I'll help.'

'This will get us into a lot of trouble, won't it?' Simon jotted down a few more symbols on his pad, then frowned and scored them out again.

'Only if we're caught.'

'Simon. If you never got into trouble you wouldn't *be* in here.' Cruikshank sat up on the bed, interested despite himself.

'Point taken. Count me in then.'

'Aye, me too.' Diddy Dave glanced across at Cruikshank. 'What about you, blondie? Gonnae be sociable for a change?'

'It depends how feasible this plan is.' Cruikshank lay back on his bed and put his hands behind his head.

'Yir a moany wee bampot, Crooky, know that?'

'I'll try being nicer if you try being prettier.'

'Go on then, Hicksy,' Dave urged. 'Tell us how you think you're gonna get aff the base.'

Jimmy grinned.

'We're going to have some unexpected help,' he said.

10.05

'You know the great thing about the virtual simulations they develop in this place?' Jimmy Hicks stood up and beckoned to the other boys. 'They're so realistic it's hard to tell them from the genuine article.'

'That's gen-up,' Diddy Dave leered. 'If I had wan o' those machines I'd program in maself, Christina Aguilera, a desert island, and nae boat.'

'Let me show you something.' Jimmy opened a door in the corner of the dormitory and stepped into the 'project room'. The other boys followed him.

The project room was a large laboratory used solely by the children. During the day, when they weren't working on one of Pinegrove's existing projects, the lab functioned as a classroom. On one wall was a huge whiteboard covered in equations and next to that an equally large computer screen. The centre of the room was criss-crossed by benches covered in test tubes and glass vials. They each had their own bench and workstation, complete with computer.

The children were encouraged to pursue their own scientific projects in the spare time they had—not that there was much else for them to do. They were supplied with any equipment and materials that the other labs weren't using—though nothing flammable or combustible was allowed. Cruikshank had blown up his father's garden shed when he was seven.

Jimmy switched on his computer and began tapping keys. Dave and Barn sat down next to him but Simon drifted over to the corner of the lab where a piece of apparatus shaped like a turbine engine rested on a bench. He hunkered down and began writing formulas in his book again. Diddy Dave glanced across.

'You back at that nippy thing? It's never gonnae work, man, know what I'm saying?'

Simon frowned and kept writing.

The 'Machine' was his pet project, almost an obsession, and he spent all *his* spare time on it. Though all the kids had dabbled with the Machine at one time or another, only Simon believed it might actually work.

The Machine was an apparatus the children had designed to send an object through time.

10.07

'Ever wonder how they train the personnel here?' Jimmy Hicks asked his companions. 'They use simulations. Stands to reason, really.'

He hit a button on his computer and the screen on the wall fizzed into life. It was suddenly filled by the image of Major Cowper, head of base security. Cowper was a formidable looking man, with shoulders like an ox, bristling black eyebrows, and a moustache to match. Barn and Dave gave a start.

'What have we done wrong this time?' Barn whispered.

Jimmy put on a headset with a small microphone attached and spoke quietly into it. As he was talking he began to type quickly on his computer keyboard.

'Barn! Diddy Dave!' The major beamed at the horrified kids. 'How would you like to come over to my quarters tonight? We can watch *The A-Team* on the television set and I'll show you my collection of bullet-proof vests.'

Simon looked up from his notebook, eyes wide. Dave shook his head in disbelief.

'You're havin' us on, man. I mean, Major Cowper, sir.'

A slow smile was spreading across Barn's face.

'That's not Major Cowper, is it?' he said. 'He's never that nice.'

'Good lad, Barn. You're right—it's a virtual simulation.' Jimmy Hicks removed the microphone, tapped a button, and the image froze, a manic grin still on its face. Diddy Dave gave a shudder.

'I found this image on an old database.' Jimmy smiled. 'It's a simulation they used to run when they were training security personnel.'

'They probably stopped 'cause Cowper's face was frightening the staff.'

'That's the whole point. A few tweaks and you can't tell it from the real person.' Jimmy turned back to his console and typed some more. On screen the chief of security seemed to materialize next door in the children's dormitory.

'He's right opposite mah bed, man,' Dave wailed. 'That's freaking me out.'

'That's exactly where I want the Ops Centre to think he is,' Jimmy said, putting the headset back on. 'I set up some transmitters that will allow us to broadcast his image right onto their screens.'

Major Cowper came to life again but now his unnatural grin was replaced by the security chief's normal dour expression. Jimmy Hicks spoke into the microphone and the major's lips moved in synchronicity with his own.

'Cowper here.' The voice was also indistinguishable from the real thing. 'My men have reported a possible anomaly in some of the security coding systems. I need you to shut down the cameras in the West Wing for a couple of minutes then bring them back online. See if that does the trick.' He tapped the console and Cowper froze.

'Put him in a tutu an' make him break-dance, Hicksy! I'd pay serious coin tae see that.'

'I can make him do or say whatever I want.' Jimmy grinned. 'It's like having the real security chief on our side.'

'You are *kidding* me!' Simon had overcome his incredulity enough to finally speak. 'You will *never* get away with this!'

'Cowper will kill you,' Barn agreed.

'He's never going to find out.'

'You better hope so, man.' Dave was still envisaging outlandish costumes for his adversary to wear. Major Cowper was not popular with the boys. As Head of Security, he was against the idea of children on a military base and made no secret of his opinion. In fact, he seemed to be against children in general.

'So what do *we* do to help?' Simon asked.

Jimmy opened a drawer and pulled out a handful of tiny devices, identical to those he had planted in the corridors earlier.

'These receive signals from my computer and boost them. Place one near any transmitting or receiving equipment on this base and I can affect it.' He handed them one transmitter each. 'Hide these on yourselves somewhere. You'll all be outside at some point today, even if it's just for exercise. Plant one wherever you can get away with it. The wider coverage we have the more places Major Cowper can crop up.'

'That's a frightening thought,' Cruikshank said laconically.

'I have a few more things to arrange.' Jimmy flicked the hair from his eyes and switched off the computer. The screen on the wall went blank. 'But Operation *Go-On-My-Date* begins at six o'clock sharp.'

'Aye, aw' right, General Patton.' Dave rolled up his sleeve. 'Ye want us tae synchronize our watches?'

Cruikshank goggled at the gold-plated timepiece the size of a small sundial on Dave's wrist.

'Where did you get *that* thing? Off the front of Big Ben?'

'Dinnae diss ma bling, bawheid.'

'Sure we'll synchronize our watches. We're in the army, aren't we?' Jimmy Hicks smiled a thin smile and for a moment he looked far more like a soldier than a kid. 'Let's show them how a *real* military operation should be run.'

11.00

Jimmy Hicks and Lesley sat in Pinegrove's canteen. It wasn't a very romantic location. Naked strip lights sputtered overhead and glass-fronted vending machines lined the walls. Half a dozen posters gave warnings about the disposal of hazardous materials and a big red board proclaimed that today's special was *Scotch Pie and chips*. Everything else was painted army regulation olive. A few dispirited sprigs of holly dangled from the ceiling in a vain attempt to give the place a festive atmosphere.

At this time of the morning the canteen was almost deserted. Two squaddies silently drank coffee in the far corner. Near the door a group of men and women in white lab coats devoured sandwiches while talking to each other in urgent whispers.

'Why the hell is the inside of the *canteen* painted olive?' Jimmy Hicks said. Under his wavy fringe, his face was long and solemn.

'There's no need to get upset about it, Hicks.' Lesley grinned and sipped her milkshake. 'Soldiers like olive. It's trendy as well as good camouflage.'

Lesley had her own kind of uniform, Jimmy thought—ripped black jeans, combat boots, a black T-shirt, and leather armbands. If it weren't for a

dyed stripe of crimson in her bobbed black hair—
and the fact that her T-shirt usually had a picture
of a Thrash Metal band on the front—she would
have passed as a member of a covert night operation. But Lesley was a teenager, like himself.

'Hey, Hicks,' his prospective date sniggered. 'If
you have pasta and antipasto for lunch, do they
cancel each other out?'

'You've got a very sunny disposition for a Goth.'

'Goths vanished in the mid nineteen-eighties.'
Lesley glanced dismissively down at her sombre
attire. 'I'm just me. I don't fit into a category.'

She looked at him over the rim of her drink
and fluttered long dark lashes in mock modesty.
Behind the thick eyeliner, her huge almond eyes
made Jimmy's heart leap.

'Tonight is still on?' she asked.

'Tonight is still on.' Jimmy glanced around but
nobody was showing the slightest interest in them.
Then again, who paid attention to a couple of
kids sharing a milkshake, even if they were hyper-
intelligent?

'I'll be glad to get out of this place, even if it's
only for twelve hours,' Lesley said enthusiastically.

'Me too,' Jimmy said solemnly. 'You have no
idea.'

Something in the way he said it made Lesley
pause. She took the milky straw out of her mouth.

'How *did* you end up here? You've never told
me.'

Jimmy sat back and thought. He seemed unsure
where to start.

27

'There was a bully at my school, used to pick on me all the time,' he said after a pause. 'He was called Frank Nitty.'

'That's the same name as a Chicago mobster from the nineteen-seventies.'

'I doubt Frank was aware of the irony.' Jimmy shrugged and lowered his head. 'I don't really like to talk about it.'

'Did I tell you my dad was an ex-soldier?' Lesley asked, although she knew she hadn't. 'He got wounded three times in the Falklands and even won a medal. Then he became a fishmonger.'

'My father was a sports nut.' Jimmy scratched his lip. 'But I could calculate precise angles in my head, so it was easy to beat him at football and basketball and pool and baseball and putting and darts. He got so frustrated he once challenged me to an arm-wrestling competition.'

'Did you win?'

'I was nine.' Jimmy stared at his palms.

Lesley reached out and took one. The boy looked surprised.

'You want to arm wrestle?'

Lesley smiled shyly. 'I want you to hold my hand. There are too many secrets in this place as it is.'

Jimmy reached out and took the slim white hand.

There was a small metallic disk hidden against her palm.

Lesley gave a grin at his surprise. The boy closed

his fingers round the object, feeling lines of circuitry embedded in its smooth surface.

'Will the disk work?'

'It should. May-Rose made it.'

May-Rose shared the other dormitory in Pinegrove with Lesley—they were the only two occupants of the girls' ward.

'Thank her for me.' Jimmy gave a frown. 'Where is May-Rose, anyway?'

'I don't know. I haven't seen her since yesterday.' Lesley leant forwards, keeping her voice low. 'For the past few days she's been totally guarded about the research she's been doing. I think she's working on something secret.'

'Lesley, everything here is secret.'

'I think she may be working in Bunker Ten.'

The boy couldn't hide his surprise. 'But that's *the* top security zone.'

Bunker 10 was the base nickname for the furthest, deepest lab on Pinegrove's lowest level. There was the usual whispered gossip about strange viruses and genetic engineering but nobody really knew what the team down there were up to. They rarely came out and, when they did, only talked to each other.

'Why would they have May-Rose down *there*? She's only twelve. The youngest of us all.'

'She's awful smart. And she doesn't cause any trouble.'

That was true. May-Rose was an illegal immigrant from Cambodia, whose family had fled government oppression and sought sanctuary in the

UK. When the British authorities had refused their request for asylum, the military stepped in and gave her parents an agonizing choice. Enrol their brilliant daughter at Pinegrove or have her sent back to Cambodia.

'You know,' Lesley said suddenly, 'I've never asked the others how they came to be on the base either. I guessed it might be a sore point.'

'None of them talk about it much,' Jimmy conceded. 'I know the army recruited Barn because of his mathematical ability. He's got muscles like Popeye, but he wouldn't hurt a fly—and the kids at his school bullied him. His parents thought he'd be better off here, but I know he misses home. Simon I'm not sure about, but I think his parents are dead. He's never said why he's at Pinegrove and I guess it's none of my business. Dave grew up on one of the toughest housing estates in Glasgow. He's just glad to be out of there.'

The boy sighed.

'I hate to admit it but they probably got Cruikshank because he's a born troublemaker.'

'Not like you, eh?'

And Jimmy Hicks suddenly felt very guilty. He tipped over the ketchup bottle and spun it on the table.

'One day in maths class,' he said quietly, 'I picked up a chair and hit Frank Nitty across the side of the head. I worked out the angle and velocity in my mind to cause maximum damage—the blow shattered his cheekbones and nose. I did it in front of the teacher so that I'd be hauled off to the head straight away and his mates couldn't get me back. Nobody ever bullied me at school again.'

He withdrew his hand, sliding the disk into his own palm.

'In fact, nobody talked to me at all.'

He slipped the device into his pocket. There were no witnesses. The soldiers were gone and the lab coats were quietly tucking into bowls of green jelly. They looked exhausted. A fat technician with a bushy beard gave a loud belch.

Lesley reached out and took his hand again.

'A year ago a Staff Officer Hutcheson arrived at my house,' she said. 'He asked if I'd ever thought of following in my father's footsteps. I said not literally, as my dad had a tendency to get shot.'

She laughed awkwardly at the memory.

'He told me I had an astonishingly brilliant mind. He said there was a special teaching facility in a place called Pinegrove where "exceptional" children were taught. That I'd receive an education to rival the finest private schools in Britain and, when I was old enough, I'd get a place at Oxford or Cambridge and my studies would be paid for.'

Jimmy gave a short laugh. 'I got Warrant Officer Mathis. He told my parents I'd be given proper discipline. A stable and controlled environment, he called it. In return I was to help with the scientific research going on at Pinegrove.'

'And agree to five years of military service as a researcher after graduating,' the girl joined in.

'And have my entire family sign the Official Secrets Act.' Jimmy took a deep, shuddering breath.

'My mother was out shopping with my sisters. They hadn't invited me.' Lesley gave a sad smile. 'They never invited me. My father said going into the army would be a huge mistake. He said he only joined to get away from his parents and his boring life.'

She fidgeted uneasily with her short dark hair.

'But that sounded like exactly what I wanted—so here I am. God knows I never thought I'd follow in my dad's footsteps.'

'For a couple of geniuses, I get the feeling we were played for suckers.' Jimmy was still smiling, but there was no humour in his eyes. 'For a few thousand pounds and a signature, the army get some of the finest minds in the country working for them for years. They think they got it made.'

'Like I say, Hicks, no point in seething about it. Hey, did you get me a Christmas present, by the way? I want something practical and yet romantic.'

Jimmy reached out and touched Lesley's cheek.

'I did. Snowshoes. But they double as earrings.'

'Good deal.' Lesley finished her milkshake with a loud slurp and gave Jimmy a mischievous wink. 'I better get *something* from you. Santa doesn't visit bad girls, you know.'

She slid off her seat.

'See ya later.'

Jimmy watched her flounce out of the door.

'I tell you,' he muttered to the ketchup bottle, 'the whole of the British army couldn't keep me in this place tonight,'

NOON

The line of olive trucks sped through the mists of Glen Isla valley. Mountains rose vertically on either side of the narrow road, sealing it in shadow. The trucks were going as fast as the treacherous conditions would allow.

In the lead cab, Lieutenant Dunwoody was now trying to read a map, following the convoy's route with a thin finger that bounced and slid across the paper. The driver risked a glance at his superior.

'Any luck, sir?'

'It would help if the damned place was *on* the map.'

'Wouldn't be much of a secret base if it was, sir.'

The lieutenant scowled at his subordinate and peered out of the rattling window.

'There,' he said suddenly. 'On the right.'

Hidden behind a rocky outcrop was a small turn-off, not much more than a track, winding into the heart of the bleakest, steepest peaks. The driver nodded and hauled at the wheel, swerving the truck onto the trail. In the following vehicles, soldiers were flung against each other and tyres squealed as the other drivers took the same course. The men held on to the seats, guns poking between their legs. Through a hole in the canvas they could see the winter sun flashing behind the snow-laden trees. Unlike army regulars these troops were dressed in jet black combat fatigues and none of them wore identification tags.

In the third truck, Private Kruger leaned across to the burly NCO sitting opposite.

'Are they trying to kill us, Sarge? What the hell's the hurry?'

The sergeant indicated out of the back of the truck. Behind was some kind of armoured carrier, a cross between a tank and a tanker. Neither man had ever seen a design like it before, but it held the road as if it were defying gravity.

'I bet it's got something to do with *that*, soldier.'

Private Kruger stared at the vehicle behind. Its windows were black-tinted slits and he narrowed his eyes in an unconscious imitation of its sinister facade.

He couldn't explain it, but something about the vehicle behind gave him the absolute creeps.

'Listen. Can you get seasick on land?' He emitted a queasy burp. 'I swear I'm going to throw up.'

'You sure that's what's making you feel ill?' the sergeant asked quizzically. The bumping of the truck gave his voice a quivery tone at odds with his stony expression.

'I'll do what I'm ordered to, Sarge.' Kruger held his superior's stare, which was no mean feat with all the bouncing around the truck was doing.

'They don't send a team like us because some

brigadier broke a nail,' the sergeant continued grimly. 'We get sent to clean up a mess. Any way we have to.'

'I'll do what I'm ordered to,' Kruger repeated. 'I always have.'

12.20

The convoy descended a steep hill and arrived at a double mesh fence, five metres high and topped with rings of vicious barbed wire. Signs every ten metres warned that this was **RESTRICTED GOVERNMENT PROPERTY.**

Each had a smaller accompanying notice.

TRESPASSERS WILL INCUR THE SEVEREST PENALTY.

The severest penalty Private Kruger could think of was death. He wondered if that was what the sign meant. It was a bad sign. Private Kruger thought he was pretty clever coming up with that, but wished he hadn't thought it all the same.

In the middle of the fence was a gate and, behind that, a thick pine forest.

The trucks ground to a halt. On a pole behind the fence a tiny camera, no bigger than a fist, scanned the small fleet. Kruger wasn't sure but it seemed to have some kind of laser attached. A group of armed men emerged from the trees and the gate slid open. Silently they checked the trucks then waved them through.

'Welcome to Pinegrove and have a Merry Christmas,' one of them said sourly.

The track led straight into the forest and the convoy followed it, rattling through the trees until the last tail light vanished from sight.

They were never to come back out.

12.28

There was a knock at the door and a lanky soldier stuck his head into the dormitory.

'Is there a Private James Cruikshank in here?'

'Naw man,' Diddy Dave piped up. 'He nipped oot fur a Chinese meal.'

Cruikshank sat up on his bed and wearily raised his hand. 'That would be me,' he said. 'And I'm not a private. I'm only fourteen.'

'Can you come with me, Private? I mean, *Mr* Cruikshank.'

Cruikshank gave his companions a mystified glance. He rolled off the bed, and hurried after the soldier, who had withdrawn his head and was already marching down the corridor.

Diddy Dave and Simon looked at each other.

'You think Cruikshank is in some kind of trouble?' Simon suggested.

'Nah. He's a wee boot-licker. He'd murder his own granny if a High Heid Yin asked him tae.'

'Still, it's a bit funny.'

'You know what's funny?' Barn was standing beside the window. 'There's a bunch of trucks just pulled into the compound. They're escorting some kind of . . . I don't know. I've never seen anything like it.'

The other boys scurried over to the window and

looked out. The area in front of their building was ringed with olive trucks, the bullet-shaped armoured carrier in the middle. Beside each vehicle, a group of soldiers stood to attention. They weren't wearing the normal camouflage of the base guards. Instead they were dressed in black uniforms and caps—more like a SWAT team than a regular army unit.

As the children watched, the reinforced doors of Pinegrove's Administration Building opened and a detachment of the base's own troops marched out to join the newcomers. The officers saluted each other and swapped identification papers. One began talking animatedly to the other but the children couldn't hear anything. The dormitory's smoked windows meant that the soldiers couldn't see that they were being watched, but the reinforced glass blocked any noise coming from outside.

'Can't you lip-read, Simon?'

'From two hundred yards away?'

'Mebbe there's gonna be a party,' said Dave pointing at the carrier. 'That big van there looks like a fridge wi' wheels. You think it's carryin' booze as a festive treat for the sodjers?'

'Sure, Dave,' Simon said. 'Maybe they've brought Christina Aguilera to do a Christmas concert.'

'I did put that on mah list tae Santa.'

Jimmy Hicks frowned. 'These guys don't look in a party mood. They're wearing full battledress.'

The officers turned and marched towards the carrier. At their signal a door opened in the vehicle's massive side. A forklift truck emerged from the shadows of the Administration Building and whizzed into the circle of vehicles—a group of men in blue overalls running alongside.

'Look, man. They've called in Kwik-Fit.'

'Will you be quiet for once, Dave?'

Within seconds the overalls had manhandled a metal and glass case out of the carrier and onto the prongs of the forklift. It reversed, slowly now, and carefully inched its way back to the complex—the men in blue walking on either side.

'Something very peculiar is going on.' Simon took off his glasses and wiped them on his sleeve. 'We've been here almost a year, right?'

The others agreed.

'In all that time have you ever seen *anything* delivered?'

'No. Unmarked trucks leave Pinegrove at night and bring back supplies the next evening.'

'Look at these guys.' Jimmy Hicks tapped the glass softly. 'They're holding on to their weapons as if their lives depended on it.'

He looked curiously at the others.

'They're ready for action.'

12.35

Cruikshank strolled back through the door, unaware of the commotion outside.

'I've got a meeting with the base commander,' he said. 'He's going to brief me and give me clearance to enter Bunker Ten.' Though he tried his best to hide it, he was fairly glowing with pride. 'They're working round the clock down there,' he continued. 'Some big project that can't wait. Need all the help they can get.'

'They probably want to test some infectious disease on you,' Simon grunted.

'Nah, they'll be needin' someone tae make the cups of tea, man,' Dave added with a laugh.

Cruikshank ignored them. Barn glanced across at Jimmy Hicks, puzzled.

'If it's something important, why didn't they ask you?'

Jimmy Hicks shrugged, envisioning the dark work that might be going on down there. 'Maybe it's because I've got a conscience.'

Cruikshank turned slowly and stared at him.

'Just what do you think you're *doing* here?' he said slowly. 'You think you're going to find a cure for cancer or something? Not in *here*. Not if you can't strap it to the front of a bomb and kill someone with it.' An unpleasant satisfaction had crept into his voice.

'The army are using us to further their aims, Hicks. I've got no problem using the army to further *mine*.'

He flopped down on his bed, stuck on his iPod and gave Jimmy a sarcastic grin.

'And they say *you're* the smart one.'

PART 2

13.00 hours—*17.00* hours

Researchers inspecting the genetic code of rats, mice and humans were surprised to find they shared many identical chunks of apparently 'junk' DNA . . .

But what the DNA does, and how, is a puzzle.

BBC News

Genetic Pollution: The spread of altered genes from genetically engineered organisms to other, non-engineered organisms.

Oxford English Dictionary

13.00

Two prospectors dropped Sherman off at the clearing in the forest and gave him one last warning about the bear.

'Grizzly come this far down the mountain in dead of winter can only mean one thing,' the younger digger said. 'Gotta be starving.'

His older companion stared at the tree tops. 'Sure, t'ain't no ordinary bear,' he said with a weary sigh that ruffled his handlebar moustache. ' 'Tis too big and 'tis too smart. 'Tis king of the bears, I'm thinking.'

'I don't care if it's queen of the damned fairies.' The younger prospector peered nervously into the thickening gloam as he unloaded Sherman's provisions. 'It's getting dark and something's sure spookin' these horses.'

He climbed back up to the comparative safety of his buckboard.

'You should come back with us, mister. You wouldn't be the first stranger that critter has killed this winter.'

Sherman handed over the last of his money.

'Thanks, but I'm actually looking for the bear,' he said.

'Well, ain't that a happy coincidink,' the youth sniffed. 'I'd lay odds at Faro the damned bear is looking for you too.'

13.30

As it was the festive season there were no classes, so the children were working on their personal projects in the lab. All except Jimmy Hicks and Lesley, who were pretending to study but secretly setting up their escape. They sat side by side, their heads close together, bent over the computer, whispering and laughing.

Simon was puzzling over the Machine as always. He knelt reverently beside it, staring at the formulas in his notebook. Barn and Dave were battling it out on a PlayStation and judging by the steady stream of Glaswegian curses, Barn was winning. Cruikshank got off the bed and strolled over to Jimmy Hicks.

'Sorry about earlier, Hicksy,' he said, though he didn't sound particularly sincere.

'Yeah,' Jimmy replied tersely. 'Me too.'

'What you working on?'

'It's a virtual simulation designed to test the ingenuity of any soldier placed in it—mainly by putting them in an unusual combat situation. Whoever uses this program will only have access to antique weapons and I'm going to make their adversary a starving grizzly bear.'

'Nice.'

On the computer screen was a forest of pines,

pristine snow stretching away between the trees. 'Low temperature, thick forest, makeshift weapons,' Jimmy said proudly. 'It's as much a survival exercise as anything.'

Cruikshank was staring at the screen.

'Those woods look familiar. Where did you get the original images?' But before Hicks could answer the boy had already guessed.

'This is the area around Pinegrove, isn't it? With the buildings and the perimeter fence missing.'

Jimmy shrugged. 'Can't escape from a place like this unless you know the terrain back to front.'

'What's that?' Cruikshank pointed to a crumbling ring of stones, half covered in snow.

'An old well—it's in the trees not far from the back gate. I think there was a croft or a small farmhouse there before the army took the place over.' Jimmy zoomed in on the pile of stones. 'It's pretty deep but they sealed the bottom with concrete.'

'In case enemy frogmen managed to swim here all the way from the North Sea?' Cruikshank said scornfully.

'The army don't like to take chances, I suppose.'

'Then they should never have let *you* in here.'

The boy gave a short laugh and went back to his bunk.

14.30

Whether it was royal or not, the king of the bears seemed to have outsmarted Sherman.

He had erected a rough lean-to of pine branches in the centre of a large clearing, hammered down the snow inside, and put his provisions on top of an oilcloth. He had carefully built a fire and then edged as close to it as he could. He didn't know what the temperatures dropped to here, but he was sure it was well below freezing.

He sat motionless for the next hour, watching flickering heat kink the air above the fire, an ancient Sharps rifle in one hand and a cup of bitter black coffee in the other. His eyes were never still, scanning the edge of the forest, looking for the deadly creature.

Even so, when it came, it arrived from nowhere.

Sherman had never seen a grizzly bear, except in pictures, and he didn't know how fast they could move. But any predator would have to cross the forty metre gap of the clearing without cover, no matter which direction it arrived from. That ought to give him time for a good shot.

And one shot was all he would get. He had a rusty Colt .45 tucked in his belt but he doubted a handgun, no matter how large, could bring down a charging grizzly. He'd purchased a couple of glass bottles, a small keg of blasting powder, and some fuse wire in the hope of concocting some kind of primitive hand-grenade—but he couldn't figure out how to make a trigger.

That left the Sharps rifle—the purchase which had taken most of his money. It was a powerful and accurate gun for its time but it could only be fired once, then it had to be reloaded using a powder cartridge and a ball rammed into the muzzle with a rod. If he missed his target he doubted he'd have time to do all that before the creature reached him.

Sherman shook his head and sighed, crystalline fog puffing between his already cracked lips.

'Give me one simple Pierson automatic laser sighted pistol,' he muttered. 'Bear would be in the happy hunting ground in ten seconds.'

He reached across and stoked the fire. When he looked back towards the trees a huge shape was halfway across the gap and loping towards him, a powdered trail drifting behind like the wake of a destroyer.

Fighting rising panic, Sherman hefted the rifle to his shoulder, took careful aim at the great plunging head, and fired. The dark mass crumpled into the snow with a grunt and slewed to a halt—its undignified collapse obscured by an explosion of sparkling white. One thin knobbed leg stuck straight into the air then slowly sank, glittering, back to earth.

Sherman already had his gloves off and the paper cartridge between his teeth when it registered what

49

he was actually looking at. He may not have seen a bear in the flesh, but he knew they sure as hell didn't have long thin legs. The creature lying in the snow gave a distressed lowing sound. Sherman was fairly certain that a grizzly, even injured, wouldn't sound as pathetic as that.

There was a snapping of branches at the edge of the clearing and the bear broke cover in exactly the same place as the moose it had been chasing. It thundered towards the dying animal but there was no doubt in Sherman's mind what the real quarry was. Sure enough, the grizzly surged past the prone moose, saliva arcing from slack black and pink jaws, tongue lolling over knife-sized fangs, heading for the lean-to.

Sherman dropped the empty Sharps and ran.

The bear was twenty metres away and gaining fast when he drew the Colt from his belt. He fired four shots, twisting as he ran, never slackening his pace. The revolver bucked violently with each shot, its bullets whistling harmlessly into the night—but it was enough to startle the huge predator, which veered off at an angle and headed, grunting, back for cover.

Sherman plunged into the trees, thrusting away the branches that whipped his face and snagged on his clothes. He burst onto a narrow deer track and sprinted along it, his breath whooshing in milky bursts. He stumbled over tree roots and hidden burrows until common sense told him that this was a suicidal course to take. Flinging himself into the undergrowth, he collapsed against a tree trunk, clutching the Colt in both shaking hands. He quickly checked the chambers.

Two bullets left. The rest of the ammunition was back in the lean-to. So were his gloves.

There was no sign of the bear.

15.25

Simon stood up, blinking rapidly. He stared at the others in the project room as if in a daze.

'Dave. Will you come and look at this?' He walked quickly to the whiteboard, wiped it clean and began writing a mass of equations. 'Please. I think I'm on to something here.'

'No can do, wee man!' Dave yelled. 'I'm kickin' some fat boy arse.'

'I just shot you,' Barn said pleasantly.

'Oh, no! I dinnae . . . stupid game, anyway.' Dave struggled to his feet and came over to the whiteboard.

'You're gonnae give yourself a breakdown working on this dippit idea,' he told Simon, bending round the still scribbling boy to see what he was setting down. 'If Einstein or Niels Bohr or Schrödinger couldnae get round the time travel problem then neither can . . . ' His mouth dropped open as he scanned the last lines of notations. Cruikshank hauled himself lazily off his bed once more and wandered over.

'What crazy theory has he come up with this time?'

Dave removed his hat. His mouth was still open. Cruikshank followed his eyes, racing across the jumble of numbers and signs.

'Oh my God,' he whispered.

15.30

After an hour sitting silently Sherman could no longer feel his hands. He tucked the gun back in his waistband, unfastened his thick hide coat and tried to warm his fingers by jamming them into his armpits. It did no good. Finally he got up and began to tramp up and down on the spot in an effort to keep warm.

He rubbed at his temple to see if he could feel his face. Clumps of frozen eyebrow came off in his hand. He started to cry and the tears solidified on his face. Another hour in these temperatures and he knew he would be dead.

With a sob he climbed back on to the deer track and headed towards the rim of the clearing.

15.34

The children were clustered round the whiteboard, gazing at the mass of tangled equations.

'Excuse my ignorance,' Lesley said. 'But my speciality is electronics and computer programs. I don't even know what I'm looking at.'

'Me neither,' Barn said. 'The maths seems right. But . . . er . . . I don't know what it means.'

Simon didn't care. He was so excited he would have explained what he had written to the tea lady. He turned to Barn and gripped the boy's meaty shoulders.

'According to Einstein, the closer you get to travelling at the speed of light the slower time goes, yeah?'

'You ken who Einstein is, don't you, Barn?' Dave chipped in.

'Of course I do,' Barn said scathingly. 'He had a lot of hair.'

'Let me put it this way. Suppose you were to leave Earth on a spaceship that travelled just below the speed of light. Because you're going so fast, time on your spaceship is slower than on Earth. So you come back after a year on your spaceship only to find that, on Earth, it's actually three hundred years later.'

'I don't get that either,' Barn said.

'Let me put it another way,' Simon began.

'You start explaining Einstein's theories to him,' Cruikshank interrupted, 'and three hundred years will have passed on Earth before he understands it.'

'Just trust us, Barn,' Jimmy said. 'It's been proved.'

'Since time slows down the closer you get to light speed then, in theory, it would actually *reverse* if you went *faster* than light. In other words you could travel back in time.'

'The problem is that nothing can travel faster than light, eh?' Dave added. 'Not even mah dad on his way tae the pub.'

'I had a crazy idea I've been working on,' Simon continued. 'Suppose Einstein didn't quite get the whole picture.'

'Aye, man. Einstein was bound tae be wrong. He wasnae near as smart as you, eh?'

'Even geniuses can miss something vital,' Simon insisted. 'Nothing can travel faster than light, sure, but suppose light *itself* wasn't travelling as fast as it could? What if light had some kind of internal brake that kept it at a slower speed? Suppose you found that brake and worked out how to disable it?'

Barn concentrated hard.

'Light would go faster?'

'It would go faster,' Jimmy nodded. 'Faster than it does now.'

Simon was trembling. 'I think I just figured out how to do it.'

'Simon,' Lesley said, her voice filled with awe. 'Are you saying you've proved time travel is possible?'

'If you could disable the brake and harness light at its faster speed then, yes, you could travel back in time. And if you could apply that brake more strongly, you could also go forward in time.'

Barn grinned at his companion. 'Does this mean the Machine will work?'

'No, it won't.' Simon shook his head. 'We don't have the technology in this lab to put the theory into practice.' He clenched his fists in a small gesture of triumph. 'But I bet it *can* be done.'

'Jesus, wee man. You'll win a Nobel Prize for this.' Dave was still staring admiringly at the formula.

'I'm going to call it "Stripped Light".' Simon turned to the others. 'Help me get this written down on the computer before the whiteboard gets hit by lightning or this place blows up or something.'

'That's hardly likely.'

'I'm not taking any chances.' Simon clutched the notebook to his chest and ran back into the dormitory, plonking himself down at his console. The others quickly followed, clustering round the ecstatic youngster.

All except Cruikshank, who was still staring, transfixed, at the board.

'To hell with the Nobel Prize,' he muttered, scanning the mass of calculations. 'This thing is worth an absolute fortune.'

15.58

The fire in the clearing was reduced to glowing embers and there was no sign of the bear. Sherman had little doubt, however, that it was close by. He tried to get the pistol out of his belt but his fingers wouldn't even move, never mind curl round the stock. He had to reach the fire and warm himself before it went out.

Sherman launched himself out of the trees and began to run towards the lean-to. After a few seconds his frozen legs gave way and he crumpled into a heap. Crying uncontrollably he began to crawl. With each thrust his uncovered hands sank into the snow, spreading the numbness past his wrists and into his forearms. Stumbling, cursing, and sobbing he threw himself forwards, pulled himself upright, and flung himself forwards again.

Finally he collapsed beside the fire, holding his hands as close to its glowing heart as he dared, until smoke began to form around his fingers. Agonizing pains shot through the backs and up his wrists but he gritted his teeth and kept them centimetres from the radiant wood. Sherman pulled the gun from his belt using his palms and tried to hold it. It dropped through his worthless hands into the snow.

There was a bellow from the edge of the forest as the grizzly emerged from the trees and headed towards him. Sherman trapped the gun in the crook of his knee and tried to cock the hammer using the palm of his hand—but the revolver kept slipping away. He forced one finger over the trigger with his other hand but knew immediately there was no way it could pull it, even if he had been able to point the weapon.

The bear had covered three quarters of the distance between them.

Sherman scuttled over to the powder barrel, raised himself up and brought both elbows crashing down on the top. The wood splintered. He did it again. The bear steadily closed the gap, never making a sound. Its face showed no anger. There was no malice in its black eyes. Only simple determination to reach its victim and tear it apart.

At the third try the snow-spoiled lid of the keg broke. Sherman scooped up a burning stick from the fire and plunged it into the shattered top. As the bear reached him and a claw-tipped arm cut into his chest, a ball of white-hot flame engulfed the lean-to and blasted them both into oblivion.

16.00

Lesley, Simon, and Jimmy Hicks were playing baseball a few hundred metres from the main buildings of Pinegrove, in a scrubby triangle of grass laughingly known as the exercise yard. Beyond that, a yellow painted line marked the furthest point that unauthorized personnel were allowed to stray from the main compound. Behind the line was a hundred metre stripe of grass and, after that, a swathe of forest with a lookout tower visible above the tops of the trees.

This was the location of the secondary gate, much smaller than the main one and the only other exit from Pinegrove. As well as the tower, it was guarded by laser-topped cameras and a lock that could only be activated by a constantly changing security code.

'What the hell are we doing?' Simon was almost apoplectic. 'I've just made one of the major scientific breakthroughs of all time, and we're out here for a *ball game*?'

'You're just scared of getting beaten by a girl.' Lesley wiggled the bat at him.

'I should be in there doing calculations!'

'Will you calm down?' Lesley continued breezily. 'You're as uptight as Hicks here. You could run a power station off his latent anger.'

Simon blinked in surprise.

'She reads too many women's magazines.' Jimmy tossed him the ball. 'What you've done is brilliant, Simon. But it's Christmas Eve and none of the top technicians are around—they're all concentrating on whatever is going on in Bunker Ten.'

'You're up first, Jimmy. Try not to trip over your own explanation.' Lesley handed the boy her bat.

'We should tell *someone*, at least,' Simon said stubbornly. 'This is important to me.' He pointed a finger at Jimmy Hicks. 'And what if your escape attempt screws this up?'

'Lesley.' Jimmy ignored the accusation. 'You throw.'

The girl fetched the ball back from Simon, who was still absently holding it by his side. Jimmy took up a stance, legs apart. Lesley swung her arm behind her head and let fly with a near perfect pitch. Even Simon was momentarily distracted.

But Jimmy made no attempt to strike and the ball whistled past his head, landing several yards away and bouncing across the torn grass.

'I've been practising,' Lesley whooped, running after the baseball. Jimmy turned quickly to Simon.

'Listen. How do *you* think the military will react to a thirteen-year-old boy wiping the floor with their top scientists, not to mention beating Einstein at his own game?' He looked round to make sure nobody in uniform was within earshot. 'You think they want that kind of publicity focused on Pinegrove?'

'Heads up!' Jimmy Hicks spun round as Lesley unleashed another sizzling throw. The ball whipped between him and Simon, almost taking the boy's glasses off. Jimmy let it go.

'What Hicks is trying to say is that we're *all* in trouble.' Lesley came running past, grinning in mock triumph.

'She's awfully cheerful for a Goth.'

'I think they call them Moshers these days, or Emo kids or something.' Jimmy's expression became serious. 'She's right, though. The military advantages of faster-than-light travel are incalculable. Top Brass aren't going to let you publish your findings or even *talk* about them. There's no way they'll allow you to take the credit.'

'That's not fair!'

'This is the *army*.' Jimmy took up a baseball stance once more. 'What's worse is that the rest of us know what you've done. Now we're *all* at risk. Stand back.'

Simon stumbled away, his mouth open. The ball whizzed past Jimmy once more and Lesley raced after it like some dark but happy sprite.

Simon's lip trembled and he felt hot bubbles of misery clog his throat. This discovery was *his*. Even the great Jimmy Hicks couldn't do what he had done. The army couldn't just take it away.

Only he knew they could. He clenched and unclenched his fists, fighting not to cry.

'We need to create this escape route more than ever,' Jimmy said urgently. 'It's not just an opportunity for Lesley and me to sneak off any more.

We may *all* have to get out some time soon—and take your discovery with us.'

Simon blinked back his tears.

'Ready, Hicks?' Lesley said. But there was something different about her voice.

'The same angle as the other times, only this time, twice the velocity,' Jimmy replied. 'Think you can do it?'

'I got magical hands.' Lesley grinned and rubbed the ball against her leg in preparation.

'No putting me off!'

She drew back her arm and let fly. The ball travelled faster than Simon's eye could follow, a white missile heading straight at Jimmy Hicks. He took one step back and swung with every ounce of strength his arms could muster. The bat connected with a nerve-jangling crack and the ball arced up and away into the sky. Simon gave a gasp as it sailed over the tops of the trees and vanished into the forest.

'Nice shot.' Lesley trotted over and gave Jimmy a kiss.

'It's all in the angle.'

'There's one of your transmitters inside that ball, isn't there?' Simon said suddenly.

'What makes you say that?'

Simon pointed to the spot where the baseball had come down.

A hundred metres further, in exactly the same direction, was the lookout tower guarding the back gate.

16.10

Sherman's eyes shot open. He was lying on a soft pallet in an empty room. A woman in a white lab coat stood beside his head. Sherman grabbed her arm and she let out a small squeak.

'I need a mirror,' he urged. 'Get me a mirror. Now.'

The woman pulled a compact from her pocket and held it up. Sherman peered at his reflection. A short, broad face with cropped hair, not ugly, but with grey stubble and heavy bags under crinkled eyes. Apart from an old scar on his forehead, however, the reflection was unmarked.

'My eyebrows are still there,' he said with obvious relief.

'Sherman, you deliberately blew yourself up. Your eyebrows being intact are the least of your worries.' The woman snapped her compact shut.

'The colonel wants to see you in his room,' she said in a businesslike manner. 'Right away.'

The colonel appeared to be in his mid-thirties, very young to hold such a rank. He was tall and fit with cropped grey hair and held himself ramrod straight, even sitting at his plain wide table. Sherman plonked himself in a smaller chair near the window. There was no other furniture in the room.

'What the hell just happened to me?' He didn't bother to salute. Despite his military demeanour, Sherman wasn't a soldier.

'Get a bit of a shock?'

'I've tested plenty of virtual simulations before, but absolutely nothing like that.' Sherman looked down at his body as if he couldn't believe he was still in one piece. 'Not even close. I don't even know where I was supposed to be.'

'The wilderness of Alaska, around the year 1745,' the colonel replied. 'It's pretty authentic too—there was a freeze on that year.'

'How do *you* know what Alaska was like in 1745?'

'I read a lot.' The colonel took a sip of water. 'The Alaska simulation is designed to place combatants in totally unfamiliar situations to see how they react—like fighting a bear in sub zero temperatures using only antiquated weapons.'

'The technology is stunning.' Sherman was impressed, despite himself.

'It's still being developed, but it's good, isn't it?'

'Are bears really that smart?' Sherman shuddered at the thought. 'It drove a moose into the clearing before it attacked, just to fool me.'

'Yes, the bear.' The colonel stroked a long chin. 'The bear is a new aspect of virtual programming altogether. It . . . er . . . *learns* from previous encounters, just like a real creature would. You might say it gets smarter with each simulation.'

'It just learned a new way to get beaten,' Sherman said nonchalantly.

The colonel frowned. 'Sherman, you blew yourself up along with it.'

'You told me that my mission was to kill the bear. I killed the bear.'

'You killed yourself too.'

Sherman looked evenly at the officer.

'That's what it *took*,' he said.

The colonel shook his head in exasperation. He opened a drawer in his desk and brought out an electronic chart. Sherman stayed silent. Eventually the uniformed man spoke.

'There's a new simulation we've been developing,' he said. 'A new concept entirely. Makes *Alaska '45* look like a PlayStation. We're talking of a scientific breakthrough of astonishing proportions.'

'What's a PlayStation?'

'Before your time.' The colonel made some notations on his chart. 'I've been recruiting a team to test this new simulation,' he said. 'Now I need a team leader with an . . . innovative approach.'

'You want *me* to test this new simulation?' Sherman said.

The colonel put his hands on the desk and leaned forward, narrowing his eyes as he spoke.

'I won't beat around the bush, Sherman,' he said coldly. 'You certainly wouldn't be my first choice.'

'Right. Don't spare my feelings or anything.'

The colonel pursed his lips. 'Let's just say that

unforeseen circumstances have forced me to go ahead with the test immediately—and you're all that's available at this short notice.'

He gave a disapproving grunt.

'You *do* have experience of unusual virtual simulations.'

'Yeah. I get stuck with all the wacky ones.'

'You also have a low rank among testers because you're not serious about what you do.'

'That's because none of it is real,' Sherman protested. 'No matter how loud the gunfire is or how many bombs are going off, you can't react the way you would in battle if you know you're really in a simulation.'

'Really?' The officer folded his arms. 'Then you might be in for a shock.'

'What do you mean?'

The colonel looked uncertain for the first time. 'This new experiment isn't like anything that's ever been done before,' he admitted. 'There are certain characters in the simulation that learn and develop, just like the bear. They were designed to rise above their programming, if you like. To reason. To have independent thought. They don't even know they're in a game . . . '

He was momentarily at a loss for words, as if the concept was almost too great for him. Sherman shared the feeling.

'That's impossible,' he said.

'Not any more.'

'You mean, once we're inside the simulation, there's no telling how these characters will react?'

'Exactly.' The colonel sat back.

'They're not bears are they?'

'No.'

'Then what will I be up against? German stormtroopers? Terrorists?' A quizzical smile played across his lips. 'Space aliens?'

The colonel didn't return the smile.

'Children,' he said, shutting the chart.

16.30

Cruikshank sat in the briefing room with Major Cowper and Lieutenant Dunwoody. He had reluctantly taken off his iPod headphones, although nobody was actually talking. Cowper's disapproval of the situation, however, was written all over his face.

The door opened and Commander Saunders, head of the base, entered along with a balding, pale-faced man in a lab coat. Cruikshank had never seen him before. The commander gave a perfunctory salute which was returned by Cowper and Dunwoody.

'Lieutenant Dunwoody, this is Doctor Monk.' The commander indicated the man in the lab coat. 'He's in charge of Project Flower, down on level six, and he'll bring you up to speed with what's been going on there. The lad is James Cruikshank,' he added, almost as an afterthought.

'Glad to meet you all,' Cruikshank said agreeably, smiling around.

'Project Flower is highly classified,' Cowper said, glaring at the boy. 'What we are about to tell you stays between us.' His eyes glittered with angry intensity. 'If you talk about this to anyone, you will know trouble in a way your clever little mind cannot even conceive. Do you understand?'

Cruikshank nodded.

'Say it.'

'I understand. Sir.'

'That'll do, Major,' Commander Saunders said quietly. Monk put his hands behind his back and coughed.

'What do you know about genetics, Lieutenant?' he asked Dunwoody.

'I've seen *Jurassic Park*.' The lieutenant's face was impassive. 'I'm just a soldier, sir. But you tell me what's going on in plain English and I'll understand.'

The commander and Monk exchanged a tense look. Cowper was still glowering at Cruikshank.

'To put it simply, Lieutenant, all creatures evolve,' Monk said. 'We evolved from apes, they evolved from lower mammals—we all evolved from single-celled creatures floating in the sea millions of years ago.'

The doctor unclasped his hands from behind his back, warming to his subject. 'Evolution takes a long time.'

'I follow you so far.'

'Project Flower was an attempt to speed that process up. A successful attempt, I might add.'

Cruikshank tore his eyes away from Cowper and listened to Monk with growing astonishment.

'All animals harbour what's called "junk" DNA—that's genetic material that has been switched off during the evolutionary process and

69

now doesn't seem to actually *do* anything. Let me put it in context—the function of ninety-seven per cent of human DNA is largely unknown.'

Monk looked down at himself as if annoyed to be part of such a mystery.

'We've been playing around with the idea that junk DNA could provide a reservoir from which advantageous new genes could be built.' He cast a glance over the table. 'Still with me?'

Dunwoody and Cowper nodded. Monk turned to Cruikshank. 'What about you?'

'There are also theories that junk DNA might act as a buffer against harmful mutations,' the boy said. 'They obviously have some importance, because animals as diverse as mice and humans have identical strings of the stuff.'

'He's not stupid, is he?' Monk looked approvingly at the commander. Cowper gave a heartfelt sigh but said nothing.

'As a matter of fact, we've been experimenting on the junk DNA in mice,' Monk continued. 'We were interested in taking it apart and putting it together to see if we could improve the creatures. And . . . er . . . we're fairly sure it worked.'

'In what way?' Lieutenant Dunwoody was keen to get past the science lesson and on to the reason he was here.

'One of the mice seems to be smarter than normal.'

'You mean it can go through a maze faster than others, that kind of thing?'

70

'I mean it escaped.'

Lieutenant Dunwoody narrowed his eyes. 'You'd better not be telling me I've been brought here to catch a damned mouse.'

'My men have already caught it,' Major Cowper said coldly.

'But not before it bit someone,' Monk interrupted. 'A girl called May-Rose.'

'May-Rose . . . ?' Cruickshank started, but a look from Major Cowper silenced him.

'With all due respect, sir,' Dunwoody looked round at the commander. 'I've been bitten by lots of things, including my ex-wife. What exactly is the problem?'

'As the boy pointed out, humans and mice share identical strings of junk DNA. The bite seems to have infected her on a genetic level.'

'Where is she now?' Dunwoody said, still anxious to get at the facts he thought important.

'Under observation in level six.' The commander opened the door and Cruikshank could see the backs of two armed guards. 'I'm taking you down there after the briefing so you can see for yourself.'

'Excuse me.' The boy raised his hand tentatively. 'Sorry, but you can't transfer genetic material through a bite. You just can't.'

'I know,' Monk scowled. 'At least, it *shouldn't* be possible.'

Cruikshank hesitated, afraid to push it. But why did they ask him here if they didn't want his input?

'What exactly did you do to this mouse?' he said.

Monk looked at the commander, his jaw knotting and unknotting. Saunders nodded.

'We don't know,' the doctor said miserably.

16.40

Sherman studied his team through a two-way mirror. There were three of them, sitting at the table in the colonel's office. Sherman hadn't known the mirror was a spying device. He wondered how many times *he'd* been observed in there.

There were two men and a woman in the room. The colonel pointed to the female first.

'That's Madrid.'

'Colourful name.'

'It's probably an alias,' the colonel said. 'She's been sent to "assist" us by High Command— arrived this morning.' The colonel's sarcastic tone made it clear that he was far from happy with this 'assistance'. 'Not my decision, but there's nothing I can do.'

Madrid was tall, probably taller than Sherman, with a muscular athletic body. Her face was tanned and pretty in a healthy farm-girl way and she had shoulder length, honey-blonde curls. Sherman nodded appreciatively.

'Don't let the innocent face fool you,' the colonel said. 'She's trained in counter intelligence—could probably take you apart with her bare hands.'

'What a way to die.'

The colonel grunted.

'The other two are from my personal team. Used them before to good effect.'

'In virtual games or real life?'

'Both. Tall, thin guy is Darren. Like you he's not a soldier. He's a whizz-kid with computers and electronics. A gamer. The other guy, the young one, is Nulce.'

Sherman studied the youngest team member. Nulce had a baby face and mannerisms to match. He was fidgeting in his seat, seemingly bored, his eyes flitting from Madrid to Darren.

'Nulce. That a code name too?'

'No, it's just a stupid name.'

'What does *he* do?'

The colonel raised a greying eyebrow.

'He kills people.'

16.58

Cruikshank was disappointed.

Bunker 10 had more exotic equipment than the higher levels and there was an air of mystery to it—especially the sets of sealed biohazard rooms, each one covered in warning symbols. But all in all, the deepest lab wasn't much different from the workplaces he had been using before.

Six white-coated technicians inhabited this particular area. All of them looked exhausted, bent over computers and typing furiously. In the centre of the room was a set of glass containers filled with coloured liquid—each with wires leading to a particular terminal. One container was bubbling. Dunwoody was in the corner with Major Cowper talking in low tones. Cruikshank yawned.

A fat technician, his beard dotted with crumbs, looked up from a console.

'Hey, kid. How about making us some tea?'

Cruikshank's eyes widened.

'What's one thousand, two hundred and sixty-seven times three thousand, six hundred and fifty-seven?' he asked.

'Eh?' The technician raised his hands in bewilderment. '*I* don't know.'

'Four million, six hundred and thirty-three thousand, four hundred and nineteen.' Cruikshank folded his arms. 'Why don't you make the tea and let me sit there? By the time you come back I'll have solved whatever problem seems to be causing you so much trouble.'

The technician stared at him for a long time, stroking his beard. He glanced across at Monk.

'Kid's got clearance.' Doctor Monk said neutrally. Cowper tutted again.

'Name's Olly.' The fat man beckoned the boy over. 'See this structure on the screen?'

Cruikshank sat next to him. On the computer console was an intricate spiralling structure labelled MR12.

'Looks like a DNA string. But I've never seen one like it before.'

Olly seemed impressed.

'It doesn't occur naturally. We been mixing up the junk DNA in lab mice.'

'And you're not sure what it does?'

'It's made one mouse smarter. But we don't know how or why.' The bearded technician gave a wry cough and lowered his voice. 'We're not even sure how we did it. We've tried repeating the experiment but we never get the same result.'

Cruikshank looked across to where Dunwoody and Cowper were now in a heated whispered discussion. The woman at the next console was staring at her screen as if the answer to the meaning of life might suddenly appear there. The rest of the assistants were just as intense.

'I don't want to seem naive,' the boy said, 'but I don't see the big fuss. It might take a while, but you'll figure it out. It's a mouse.'

Olly looked awkwardly at him.

'This sample isn't from the mouse. It's from the girl called May-Rose. We took it after the mouse bit her.'

'This is impossible. You can't alter someone's DNA like that. Not through a bite. Not even if it transferred blood!'

'That's what *we* thought.' Olly put his head in his hands. 'But it happened.'

Cruikshank stared at the screen, transfixed by the unfamiliar spirals studded with unknown combinations of genetic material.

'What's actually happened to May-Rose?'

'We're not sure.' Olly pursed his lips. 'She's in isolation now, under constant guard.'

'Then instead of fiddling around with your computer simulations wouldn't it be best to talk to her?'

'We tried,' Olly said slowly. 'Sent in four technicians to interview her. They're all dead.'

Cruikshank gave a start. The blonde woman at the next computer stopped typing, a look of alarm spreading across her face.

'Olly,' she whispered urgently, 'he's a kid.'

'So was May-Rose!'

'What do you mean *was*?' Cruikshank said quietly. The rest of the assistants had stopped working and were watching the exchange, faces tense and grey.

'Just leave it!' the blonde woman hissed.

'What do you think this boy is *doing* down here?' The fat technician's face had gone bright red. Cruikshank couldn't tell if it was anger or embarrassment. 'You think they asked him here for his expertise, goddammit?' He slammed his fist onto the computer keyboard. The blonde closed her eyes. The others looked quickly away.

'I'll make that tea,' Cruikshank said, a sinking feeling opening in the pit of his stomach.

'Don't have time for that, son.' Lieutenant Dunwoody walked over and laid a calming hand on Olly's shoulder. 'We're going to go and see May-Rose.'

PART 3

17.00 hours—18.00 hours

Meme: An element of culture or system of behaviour that may be considered to be passed from an individual to another by non-genetic means.

Oxford English Dictionary

17.00

The children had set up a circle of chairs in the dormitory. Cruikshank and May-Rose were both missing, presumed to be in Bunker 10. The rest leaned close together and kept their voices low.

'I say we need a plan, man.' Diddy Dave had obviously been thinking along the same lines as Jimmy. 'If the army get a scooby that we've got the secret of faster-than-light travel, they'll nick it like a shot, know?'

'What do you mean *we*?' Simon gave Dave a venomous look. 'I discovered it, remember?'

'Aye, OK. Keep yir pants on, wee man.'

'Let's all agree on one thing right away,' said Jimmy Hicks. 'Whatever happens, Simon gets the credit for this.'

The others nodded.

'The simplest thing to do is to keep quiet for the moment.' The whiteboard had been wiped clean and Simon's workings were hidden in an inoffensive file on his computer. 'And we need to hide a hard copy of the formula somewhere, so that we can use it as security.'

'Could we email it out of here?'

'To who? Anyway you can be sure the military monitors all our communications to the outside.' Jimmy beckoned them even closer. 'But there's an old dried-up well in the forest, not far from the back gate. It's deep. When Lesley and I sneak out tonight we should take a copy of the formula in a sealed bag. Drop it in there on the way out.'

Simon was silent.

'What?'

The boy looked at the ground. 'I was thinking that there's nothing to stop you from keeping the formula and not coming back.' He kept his eyes down, but his voice was trembling with emotion. 'Take all the credit.'

'Dinnae take a flaky, wee man,' Dave cut in. 'Hicksy wouldnae dae that.'

'Well, why can't we all go?' Simon was insistent. 'What if *Cruikshank* tells top brass about the equation?'

'Why would he?' Jimmy replied brusquely. 'He's selfish but he's not stupid. The army would treat him as a security risk and lock him up.' He sat down beside his friend, his voice softening.

'We need to know if this escape route will work, Simon. If Lesley and I get caught, we can tell them the truth—that we wanted to go on a date.'

'You don't really think they'd believe you,' Simon insisted.

'No. But they can't prove otherwise,' Lesley shot back. 'On the other hand, if *everyone* gets caught sneaking out, we'll be interrogated until someone breaks. You know that. Besides, we can't leave without Cruikshank and May-Rose.'

Jimmy looked into the boy's eyes.

'Simon. We're your family. Trust us.'

'Aye, ye wee bam. You're like a sister tae me.'

Simon took a deep breath.

'All right then. Let's stop wasting time and put this escape plan into operation.'

17.10

Sherman sat down for the first time with his new team. Each had a folder open in front of them, filled with maps and specifications. The colonel stood at the head of the table, hands on his hips.

'I have a big problem,' he said matter of factly. 'And it needs to be sorted right now.'

That got their attention.

'I'm sending you into a virtual combat simulation, but this one is different from any that has been created before.' He pursed his lips, choosing his words carefully. 'You're going to be immersed in it for hours and it will be more real than anything you've ever experienced. Sherman here is used to odd simulations and he'll be leading you.'

'What's our brief?' Darren asked. He had a high quivery voice that matched his meek demeanour.

'To break into a hostile military base and penetrate to its lowest level.'

'Typical game scenario, just in reverse,' Darren said approvingly, looking down at his notes. 'Difficult though. There are watchtowers back and front and you have to get past a double perimeter fence and mounted lasers just to get near the place. The lasers are tiny but they've got massive firepower and an enormous range, which makes them almost impossible to take out.'

'Is there a blind spot where we can cut through the fences?'

'No need,' the colonel said curtly. 'The lasers will be off, I'll give you the code for the gate, and the guards will be elsewhere.'

Nulce gave a small snort.

'You have a problem, Mr Nulce?'

'That's not much of a challenge.' Nulce had an American accent, but Sherman couldn't place it.

'I'm not interested in the more mundane parts of the simulation,' the colonel continued. 'The problem we have is with its integral workings.'

'Sir.' Darren looked puzzled. 'Exactly what is wrong with this simulation?'

'It's radically different from any designed before,' the colonel said. 'In fact, we went further than we could ever have dreamed.' He put his hands together and looked at his team over the tops of his fingers. 'We've learned how to create characters in the simulation that can actually evolve. They can act in ways that aren't in their programming.'

'Holy hell,' Darren breathed. 'That *is* different. I didn't think it was possible.'

'It wasn't,' the colonel said, faintly proud. 'Not until now.'

'This simulation must be worth a *huge* amount of money.' Darren's mind was reeling with the possibilities. 'Not just to the army but to big business. It has massive marketable applications for all sorts of non-military industries.'

'I'm well aware of that,' the colonel said. 'Where do you think we got most of our funding?'

'How many characters are able to act independently?' Sherman broke in.

'Seven of them. All children.'

'Sorry to have so many questions, sir.' Darren spoke up again. 'But why children?'

'This type of simulation was to be the ultimate test for soldiers.' The colonel stroked his chin, pondering the best way to drop his bombshell. 'Each child's personality is based on that of a military dictator from the past. Stalin, Hitler, Pol Pot, that kind of thing. Even the girls. And their IQ has been upped to genius level.'

'And they can really operate outside their programming parameters?' Darren said.

'They can.'

'Can I venture a guess at their purpose?'

'Be my guest.'

'These characters are supposed to learn and grow inside the simulation, aren't they?' Darren continued.

'They are. The program runs continuously.'

'If they evolve into adults, they'll be the ultimate adversaries in combat simulations. Super intelligent, utterly ruthless, and totally unpredictable. That's brilliant!'

'So what's the problem?' Madrid spoke for the first time. Her voice was hard and husky and her manner was straight to the point.

'One of the "characters" is a child called May-Rose.' The colonel held up a photograph of a pretty Asian girl with long dark hair. She was standing in front of a seafront scene, holding an ice cream.

'I'm not sure what happened really,' he said looking wistfully at the girl. 'Don't know if there was a weird short circuit or a programming anomaly.'

The team were listening intently now, intrigued and disturbed in equal measure. Everyone who had worked with him knew the colonel was no fool. It wasn't like him to admit uncertainty.

'Anyhow, whatever happened, May-Rose seems to know she's a computer program.'

'Say *what*!?' Nulce exploded.

'Pardon me, sir,' Darren said politely. 'Are you sure?'

'Pretty sure. She's turning the simulation into chaos—to the extent that we're no longer in control of it. We can't reroute the programs—we can no longer even identify *her* program. Worst of all, we can't shut the simulation down.'

'She's overriding systems?' Darren drew in a sharp breath.

'I'm not Jimmy Neutron,' Sherman said, 'but this all sounds very sinister.'

'It's downright terrifying,' Darren said quietly. 'If she's really self-aware, she may be trying to get out.'

'Eh? What's she . . . I mean *it*, gonna do?' Nulce scoffed. 'Leap outta the screen and take off down the corridor?'

'The simulation is run by a computer and that computer will be part of a computer system,' Darren said. 'Am I right, sir?'

The colonel signalled an affirmative.

'And somewhere in that system there will be access to other systems.' Darren shot Nulce a look of scorn. 'How do you think computer viruses spread?' He paused to let what he was saying sink in. 'Imagine what a virus that could actually *think* would be capable of? Do you realize what it could do if it got on to the World Wide Web?'

Madrid was staring at her commander.

'What have you done, Colonel?' she said coldly.

'We can't shut the simulation down but the mainframe computer has a built in failsafe,' the officer retorted. 'If it looks like any rogue program is in danger of subverting it, the computer will delete the simulation entirely. Wipe it from its memory.'

Darren looked cautious. 'I suggest you shut this one down right now, sir.'

'Oh, I don't think the colonel would want *that*,' Sherman commented drily. 'That would be a lot of money and research down the drain.'

'It would be an *enormous* amount,' the colonel agreed. 'And all we need is a sample of this character's program to continue our research. Problem is, we can't get at it from the outside any more.' He permitted himself a wry smile. 'That's why you're going into the simulation to get it.'

'A sample?' Sherman sounded puzzled. 'How do we do that?'

'May-Rose is a program,' Darren tried to explain. 'But in the simulation she's operating as a human. We need a sample of her.'

'What? Like an *arm*?'

'Blood. Saliva. Even skin.' Darren shrugged. 'A tiny piece of her programming is all we need to build another model of her. Like you could build a clone of someone from a string of their DNA.'

'God, I hate technology,' Sherman muttered.

'There are "samples" of all the character programs in the bottom level of the simulation—its database, if you like. The one you're looking for is labelled MR12. Your task is to find it and bring it back, overcoming resistance with deadly force.'

Nulce gave a broad smile.

'Near the perimeter fence of the base is an abandoned well. Put the sample in a lead container—it'll be part of your equipment—and drop it there. The well is a conduit point to transfer information in and out of the simulation, so I can retrieve the data from there. That's your objective. Complete it successfully and the game is over. Then I bring you out.' The colonel put his hands behind his back. 'Any questions?'

'What if we encounter these "children"?' Nulce asked. 'Do we kill them too?'

'Negative.' The colonel shook his head. 'The simulation is in chaos. You'll need their help to navigate to the bottom level.'

'Need help from a bunch of kids?' Nulce gave a nasty laugh.

'It says here their characters aren't even combat trained.' Sherman looked up from his notes. 'None of them are over fifteen.'

The colonel slammed his fist down on the table. Darren started, looking quickly up from the folder.

'Do NOT underestimate the flexibility of these new programs,' the officer warned. 'Their characters are fledgling psychopaths and they're a hell of a lot smarter than you.' He tapped the folder in front of him. 'They can't overcome you with violence so they'll use their brains—and in that department, you are *totally* outclassed.'

He looked at each member in turn, tapping the table for emphasis. 'You do NOT listen to them. You do NOT believe anything they say. And you get the sample MR12—but you do NOT get anywhere near May-Rose herself. You never, EVER let May-Rose talk to you.'

'When do we start?' Madrid said.

'In an hour.'

'Not much of a Christmas Eve,' Darren muttered.

'Yeah. We haven't had time to buy each other presents,' Nulce added sarcastically, glancing at his companion.

The colonel remained silent.

'This is all a bit odd.' Sherman sat back and looked at his superior. 'I've just met my team. We haven't had time to go over the information together.'

'With all due respect, sir,' Madrid broke in, 'I was assigned to this project by Central Command. I'm supposed to assess your progress and report back before any human testing is done.' She looked around at the others. 'I'd like a chance to look at the equipment and find out more about the team before we actually go into the simulation.

I've just arrived after a long flight and I'm tired and hungry.'

'And I have no intention of getting bogged down in red tape.' The colonel shot Madrid a look of barely suppressed hostility. 'While you're here you operate under my direct command. We go in an hour. You can make your report when your task is completed. I'll take full responsibility.'

Madrid stared at the colonel for a few seconds.

'Yes, sir,' she said finally.

'Look. I know this is all very unusual.' The officer's voice lightened a little. 'But this project is only partly military. It's heavily financed by private companies who expect a lucrative return on their investment. Those backers would pull any future aid if they knew the way this experiment is turning out.'

The hardness returned to his voice and he looked pointedly at Madrid.

'This is still *my* project and I've no intention of having it taken away from me at the eleventh hour.'

He turned his steely gaze on the others. 'To demonstrate just how important this mission is, our private investors are prepared to offer an attractive incentive.'

'I'm a soldier, Colonel,' Madrid said. 'All you have to do is order me.'

'The hell with you.' Nulce's eyes widened. 'I'll do my duty all the better if I think there's some cash involved.'

The colonel clasped his hands in front of him

and took a deep breath. 'If you can successfully retrieve a sample of MR12, each of you will be paid two million pounds. You have my guarantee. You can have it in writing if you like.'

The silence round the table was palpable. Darren gave a small cough.

'Did you say two *million*?'

'That's correct.'

'*Now* it's starting to feel like Christmas.' Nulce beamed.

All of them looked at Madrid.

'As you say, I'm under your direct command for the moment,' she told the colonel. 'And I intend to make a full report when this is over.' She gave a little shrug. 'I'll still accept the two mill, though.'

'Then get yourselves to the Infirmary.' The colonel beckoned to his team. 'They'll prep you and set you up for entering the simulation. As they say, time is money. As far as I'm concerned you're good to go.'

17.15

Cruikshank followed Olly and Doctor Monk out of the lift and into the corridors of the lowest level. Behind him were Lieutenant Dunwoody, Major Cowper, and three armed guards.

'After she was bitten, we put May-Rose in an isolation booth,' Monk said. 'We have a bio-safety level four lab with an air-locked door and a decontamination shower next door but, at the time, we didn't see any need to move her there.' He looked nervously over his shoulder. 'She seemed perfectly all right and we didn't consider any risk of infection. The team that went in to examine her were wearing gauze masks and sterile gloves but no biohazard gear.'

'What happened to them?' Dunwoody asked.

Olly and Monk had stopped at a metal door.

'You really think the boy should see this?' Olly remonstrated.

'We don't have a choice.' The commander approached a control panel on the wall and punched in a long code. Olly put his hand on Cruikshank's shoulder.

'This isn't going to be pleasant, kid,' he whispered. 'I don't even know why they brought you down here, but you hang in there, OK?'

There was a click as the locking mechanism rolled back and the door slid open.

Cruikshank found himself entering a narrow room. Facing him was a large observation booth with reinforced glass. It reminded him of the monkey house at a zoo, but without the smell.

May-Rose sat on a chair at one end of the booth, head in her hands. Behind her was a narrow bunk, attached to the wall. She didn't look up.

At the other end of the booth, four men lay on the floor, surrounded by a vast pool of congealed blood. Their lab coats had been pristine white but were now stiff and dark with gore. Cruikshank felt a thick queasy feeling rise in his stomach and Olly tightened his grip on the boy's arm.

Dunwoody stepped forward.

'What the hell did she do to these men?' he said. He tried to keep his voice steady but it was obvious that even this hardened soldier was shocked.

'She didn't do anything,' Olly broke in. 'They did it to themselves.'

'What?'

'They killed each other. They were all carrying medical kits. Scalpels, syringes, that kind of thing.'

'Can we talk to her?' Dunwoody looked at the intercom system, set beside the door.

'The intercom is broken and the booth is soundproof.' Major Cowper tapped the glass. May-Rose didn't look up. 'But you can talk to the survivor.'

'Survivor?'

'He was outside watching the other men,' said

Monk caustically. 'That's why they call it the observation booth.'

'He's next door,' Olly continued, fumbling awkwardly with his beard. 'Does the kid have to come? Hasn't he seen enough?'

'I like it less than you,' Cowper snarled. 'But we need him here.'

'Hey. The kid is standing right next to you.' Cruikshank straightened himself to his full height of five feet. 'Remember?'

He looked up at Olly, who avoided his gaze. But Cowper and Monk were staring at him. Cruikshank narrowed his eyes.

'Just why *am* I with you?' He turned and glared at Monk. 'It's obvious none of you want me here and none of you think you need my help. So what *am* I doing here?'

'Since the incident, May-Rose hasn't been able to talk to us,' Monk said. 'And we can't let her out, in case she somehow caused this . . . mess. But she has managed to communicate one message.' He walked over to the thick glass and thumped loudly on it. This time May-Rose's head shot up.

Cruikshank took a step back. May-Rose had dark, oriental eyes and he had always found it hard to tell what she was thinking. But now they were fastened on him and he suddenly didn't want to know. He really didn't want to know.

May-Rose stood up. She moved slowly towards the party, never taking her eyes off Cruikshank. She reached the glass and opened her mouth wide. He felt the hairs on his neck rise.

May-Rose breathed on the glass, five or six times. With one finger she wrote on the foggy surface, inverting the letters so that everyone on the other side could read them.

She stepped back and pointed at the boy. Cruikshank felt his stomach grow cold as he read what she had written.

NEED TO TALK TO YOU.

17.20

Jimmy Hicks sat at his computer console in the dormitory. Beside him lay a tiny walkie-talkie. Diddy Dave had spent the afternoon making one for each of them and they transmitted on low power at a frequency the army didn't use.

Jimmy picked his up and clicked a button on the top.

'Puddle Pig,' he said quietly. 'This is Swamp Rat. Are you in position? Over.'

'Puddle Pig?' Lesley's voice crackled over the other line. 'You talking to me?'

'I thought you should have a code name. Over.'

'That's a pet name, not a code name,' the line fizzled. 'I want to be called Black Mambo.'

'At the end of each transmission you're supposed to say over. Over.'

'I'm supposed to say over over?'

'Not over over. *Over*. Over.'

Lesley burst into a fit of muted laughter. There was an impatient cough from behind and Dave leaned over Jimmy's shoulder.

'Aw' right, Sergeant Bilko. Enough. Lesley doll? Where are you?'

'I'm round the back of the building. Heading through the bushes and into the trees.'

'Roger that, good buddy. That's a big ten-four

and aw' that numpty stuff. Catch ye later. Over an' oot.'

He switched off the walkie-talkie and handed it to Jimmy.

'Right. Now you do your stuff, man. Ahm dyin' tae see you pull this aff.'

Jimmy Hicks took a deep breath, bent over the computer and started typing. In the corridors of Pinegrove the tiny receivers Hicks had planted earlier began to process the information he was feeding them and transmit signals to each other.

A blue light blinked on Warrant Officer Took's console in the Operations Room. He put on his headphones and opened his com link. Major Cowper appeared on the screen in front of him.

'Took? Cowper here. I want you to listen up. Switch this transmission to a secure system.'

Took looked surprised, but did as he was told.

'I need to keep this between you and me,' Cowper said quietly. 'Don't say anything. Just listen.'

In the dormitory, Jimmy Hicks talked into a mike attached to the headphones he was wearing.

'I've detected an odd glitch in our software systems,' Hicks said. On the screen in front of him, the simulation of Major Cowper was saying exactly the same thing and the boosters sent it straight to Took's console in the Ops Room.

'I don't need half the technicians on this base trawling through the security systems, Took,' Cowper was saying. 'It's probably nothing, so let's investigate this thing in-house, before we broadcast it and get egg all over our faces.'

'Sir,' Took said quietly. 'What do you need me to do?'

Warrant Officer Took was fairly excited at the prospect of a covert operation—it would make a welcome change. His console was at the rear of the room and most of the staff had their backs to him. Took had often cursed his isolated position, but he supposed that was exactly why the major had picked him to communicate with.

'I need access to the base security systems to check this glitch out.'

'Yessir,' Took said. Then in a puzzled voice, 'Only . . . you already have access to the security systems. You're head of security.'

Cowper gave the soldier his legendary glare of disapproval.

'If there's an anomaly,' he said, voice dripping with sarcasm, 'I may not be able to spot it using computers that are in the normal loop.' Cowper stepped back and indicated the room behind him.

'So I'm in one of the dormitories where those annoying kids are billeted. Their computers, obviously, don't have access to our security systems either. I've sent all the little devils off on errands and I want you to patch one of their consoles into the main security frame. Then I can check it out from here.'

Took frowned.

'Begging your pardon, but isn't that highly irregular, sir?'

Cowper's eyes bored into the nervous man. 'Of course it's irregular, soldier. I do irregular things all the time which, surprise, surprise, you're not normally party to. That's because I'm head of security and you are a junior officer—which you will most definitely stay if I don't get some co-operation.'

'Sir. Yes, sir.'

'Now patch me through to computer four-five-seven in the kids' dorm and make sure nobody else detects it. I'll only be on a few minutes.'

Cowper reached out and the screen went blank.

'Of course, Major Cowper.' Took gave a grimace at his own stupidity and began to flip switches.

Diddy Dave was seated at his computer—number 457—a few feet from Jimmy Hicks.

'Information coming through,' he said. 'We're patched into base security.' He began to type furiously. Both boys watched him, holding their breath. After a couple of minutes he looked up.

'I've got the whole shebang,' he breathed. 'Access codes, schematics—even the routings of the internal systems.'

'Capture that info and secure it,' Jimmy said.

'Aw'ready done.'

'Good man.' Jimmy switched on his mike and began transmitting again.

Cowper appeared on Took's screen with a bleep, giving the operator a start. Took looked round but nobody was paying much attention to him. Everyone was dreaming of the Christmas they were missing and the Ops Room had a subdued, depressed air about it.

'Any progress, sir?'

'Just what I thought,' Cowper said. 'A minor fault in a sub-routine. I've bypassed it for now and I'll sort it from my own console in a couple of days. Happens now and then.' The major gave an uncharacteristic smile. 'Good work, Warrant Officer. Your co-operation and your silence is appreciated. I'll remember it.'

'Yes, sir. Thank you, sir.'

'Thank *you*, soldier.'

The screen went blank.

In the dormitory, Dave leaned back in his chair and let out a deep breath.

'Jeez.'

Jimmy swivelled round and gave his friend a thumbs-up signal. Simon, who had been watching with bated breath, finally exhaled.

'Now what?'

Jimmy Hicks turned back to his computer and picked up the walkie-talkie.

'Lesley, Barn? You there?'

'You forgot to say over.'

Jimmy grinned.

'Head for the fence. But stay a couple of hundred metres from the rear gate. Let me know when you get there.'

'Affirmative.'

'Good luck, guys.' He put the walkie-talkie down and fastened the headset tightly on his head.

'Now we go to phase two.'

17.25

'Tell us what happened, soldier.'

Major Cowper, Lieutenant Dunwoody, and the commander stood along the side of the wall like a miniature firing squad. Monk, Olly, and Cruikshank were off to one side, watching.

The observation technician sat at a bare table on the other side of the room. He didn't seem intimidated by the military powers here to interrogate him, or by the fact that his scientific boss was here as well. He stared at the uniforms opposite in a glazed way, as if he couldn't really see them. Commander Saunders cleared his throat.

'What happened to your team, soldier? Tell us what you saw.'

The observer closed his eyes. He tilted his head, as if listening for something.

'I saw my team kill each other,' he said quietly.

'Can you tell us how that came about?' Dunwoody stepped forwards. 'Run us through it.'

'They went into the observation booth. Wanted to talk to May-Rose about getting bitten by that mouse. Can I have a cigarette?'

'There's no smoking down here.'

The observer nodded. 'They took a blood sample from her and passed it out to me. Then they went back and started asking her routine

103

questions—about how she felt, that kind of thing.' The observer was sitting upright in his chair now. Very upright. As if he was trying to stay calm.

'Next thing, the team were all fighting with each other. Popper, Ince, and Wilmut turned on the team leader, Bunton. But Bunton was bigger. He killed Ince with a scalpel and strangled Popper. Wilmut kept fighting him, he's tough like a wee terrier—he and Bunton went at it until they were both dead. I hammered on the wall to try and distract them, but all I did was break the intercom.'

'You didn't go in to help them?'

'I couldn't. After seeing that . . . chaos, I knew the door had to stay sealed.'

Dunwoody glanced across at Monk.

'We have no idea what went on,' the doctor concurred. 'But we can't discount the possibility that this outburst was caused by some airborne virus. That somehow it jumped from May-Rose to the medical team. Drove them mad.'

'That's why the observation booth is still sealed with May-Rose and the team inside,' Olly agreed. 'This area isn't equipped to deal with airborne contamination.'

'And the observer?'

'Tested clean for everything. Otherwise we wouldn't be in here talking to him.'

'Lieutenant Dunwoody,' the commander broke in. 'I'll see you outside for a moment.' He stepped out into the corridor and Dunwoody followed him.

In the passageway the two armed guards

automatically moved further away. Commander Saunders shut the door behind him.

'You delivered a portable containment unit to us this afternoon,' he said. 'Now you know why. We have to assume May-Rose somehow caused the deaths of these men. Accept the possibility that she's the carrier for some kind of virus. We need to get her into that secure unit and transfer her to the biohazard labs.'

'The room she's in now isn't much more than a glorified bus shelter,' Dunwoody agreed. 'It's got sealed doors and windows but not much else by way of protection. Do you have an experienced Medvac team who can move her?'

'We do.'

Dunwoody looked evenly at him.

'You don't send men like mine to be delivery boys,' he said. 'That's not what we're trained for.'

The commander's jaw worked silently.

'Your troop is positioned on the upper levels, yes?'

'That's correct.'

'As I said, we don't know if this *is* a virus. We don't know why these men went mad. But if something goes wrong . . . ' The commander was finding it difficult to put his fears into words. Dunwoody knew why.

'If your men start going nuts,' he said, 'my soldiers will seal off the lower levels. Nobody will get out.'

The commander took a deep breath. Then he gave a sharp, practised salute.

'Go and brief your men, Lieutenant.'

17.30

Jimmy Hicks picked up his walkie-talkie and turned it on.

'Lesley. What's your position? Over.'

There was a short burst of static then Lesley's voice came over the airwaves, crisp and clear.

'Barn and I are at the edge of the woods. There's a fifty metre gap or so and then we can just make out the perimeter fence. We can see the lights of the rear guard tower. It's about a kilometre away.'

'Wait for my signal. Then walk out to the perimeter fence and shine your flashlights around.'

'Will do.'

'And make sure not to shine your beams on each other.'

'My God, you really are a genius, Hicks. I'd never have thought of that.'

'Thank you for your sarcasm, Lesley.' Jimmy gave a wide smile. 'Over and out.' He turned to Diddy Dave.

'Your turn, pal. You've got security access on your computer. Can you patch me into the communications system at the guard tower?'

'Fast as light, man.' Dave jerked a thumb at Simon. 'Even faster if owl boy's bampot theory is right.'

'Who's on duty in there tonight?'

Dave consulted the computer screen. 'Privates Jakar and Smith. They're getting relieved in a couple of hours by two soldiers called Macintosh and Watts.'

'Perfect.' Jimmy put the headphones back on and adjusted the microphone. 'Open a channel to the tower's communications system and shut down their heating. Simon?' He tossed the walkie-talkie to the smaller boy. 'You know what to do.'

In the observation tower Jakar and Smith were brewing tea. Jakar was trying to explain the rules of cricket to Smith. Smith was gazing out over the treetops and thinking that this was the kind of place Santa would live, if he existed.

The screen on their communication console flickered to life.

'Jakar, Smith? Major Cowper here.'

The two men leapt to attention and saluted.

'Easy, men,' Cowper said, with a friendly smile. 'You'll do yourself an injury.'

Jakar and Smith couldn't hide their surprise. The major wasn't the type to make jokes—even bad ones.

'I have good news and bad news,' Cowper said. 'Bad news is your heating's gone off.'

Both men groaned. It was bad enough being stuck up in this tower with nobody but each other to speak to. It would be intolerable without heat.

'Good news is, I already have Privates Macintosh and Watts out doing a routine check of the perimeter fence.'

The two guards exchanged knowing looks. That was like Cowper—sending men out on Christmas Eve to check a fence.

'Take a look out,' Cowper said. 'You see them anywhere?'

Back in the dorm, Jimmy Hicks put his hand over the mike and nodded to Simon. Simon pressed send on the two-way radio and spoke softly.

'Lesley. Barn. Flashlights on and head for the fence.'

Back in the observation tower, Jakar and Smith peered out of the window.

'No sign of anybody yet, sir,' Smith said. Jakar nudged him and pointed. 'Wait a minute. I see two flashlights coming out of the trees and heading for the fence. They're on our side, about half a kilometre away. Can't see the people, only the beams.'

'That'll be them,' Cowper said. 'Tell you what. You two get back to the base before you freeze. I'll tell Macintosh and Watts to head over once they've finished their sweep. They're dressed for a recce, so the heat being off won't bother them.'

'You sure, sir?'

'It's Christmas Eve, soldier. I may be strict, but I'm not a monster.'

'That's debatable,' whispered Smith under his breath. Jakar nudged him again, hard this time.

'Yes, sir; thank you, sir. We'll fill out our report sheets and head back. Take about ten minutes.'

'You do that.' The major reached out to switch off the channel. Then he paused.

'And listen, you two,' he said. 'You keep this to yourselves, OK. Don't want everyone on the base to think I'm a big softie.'

'Roger that, sir,' Jakar grinned.

'Cowper out.'

The screen went blank.

Simon got on the walkie-talkie again.

'The guards will be leaving in about ten minutes, you guys,' he said. 'Once they've gone, Barn can come back and Lesley, you head towards the perimeter gate. Jimmy's going to be out shortly. You've got nearly two hours before the real guards turn up. I'll pull the Cowper routine to explain to Macintosh and Watts why the guard post is unmanned when they get there. We'll do another variation tomorrow morning to get you both back in.'

'Cool. According to Jimmy there's a deserted ranger station on a hill a kilometre from the base. Once he joins me we're going to head there and build a little fire. Apparently the building is still intact and the view is spectacular.'

'You have a good time, Lesley.'

'Thank you, Simon.'

'My pleasure. Teenagers are supposed to sneak out on dates.' The boy gave a wry grin. 'It's just normally not this much trouble.'

17.45

Cruikshank was observing the observer. According to the men who found him, he'd been raving mad. He didn't look insane now, but he did seem like a tortured soul fighting to stay in control of his emotions. His jaw was twitching and he stared straight at the wall, not at his superiors. Cruikshank put his hand up. He wasn't sure what the appropriate protocol was with Major Cowper, so he thought he'd try politeness.

'Major, sir. May I ask a question?'

Cowper glared at him. Then he shrugged. The commander and this upstart Dunwoody were having private conversations in the corridor and he felt he was getting cut out of the loop. He could appreciate how the kid felt.

'Be my guest,' he said.

Cruikshank turned to the observer.

'Why did you break the intercom system?'

The observer kept staring into space. Cowper tilted his head, curious as to where this was going.

'Answer the question, soldier,' he snapped.

'I hit it when I was hammering on the door,' the observer said.

'If you were trying to attract your team's attention, why didn't you hammer on the glass?'

110

The man hesitated. 'I hammered on everything,' he said finally.

'You said the team were asking May-Rose questions,' Cruikshank pressed. 'You must have heard what she was saying. Until you broke the intercom.'

The observer looked at the security officer. 'That's more than one question, Major Cowper.'

Cowper narrowed his eyes. He was intrigued despite himself.

'Just humour the kid,' he said.

'What did May-Rose say to your team?' Cruikshank repeated.

The observer gripped the arms of his chair. Beads of sweat had appeared on his forehead.

'I don't remember.'

'We already know what you saw. What did you hear?'

'I don't know what you mean.' The observer was trembling all over. Cowper rose and took a slow step towards him, letting his hands relax and fall by his side. He knew the boy was on to something.

'What was May-Rose saying?' he repeated.

'Did she say something that made these men go mad?' Cruikshank broke in as Cowper leaned threateningly over the seated man. 'Something so terrible that you smashed the intercom before it did the same to you.'

'Please stop asking me questions.' The man's voice was harsh and cracked. 'I don't know anything.'

'What did you hear?' Major Cowper insisted.

'What did she sound like?' Cruikshank added.

The observer launched himself out of the seat, arms outstretched, straight at the boy. Major Cowper moved forwards too, fast and loose, head low and fists bunched. His shoulder connected with the observer and both spun away from Cruikshank. Monk looked stunned.

'Guards! In here!' Olly shouted.

The door burst open and the two soldiers rushed into the room in time to see the observer grab Cowper by the throat. The major slammed one hand on his opponent's face, pushing the assailant away, and his other hand scrabbled for the holstered pistol. The guards hauled the observer off and pinned him against the wall. The observer's face was a mask of frozen hate, lips pulled back over bloody teeth, snarling like a rabid animal.

'SHE HAD THE VOICE OF GOD!' he screamed, spittle dripping over his quivering lips. His knees buckled and he began to cry. Only the grip of the guards kept him upright.

'She had the voice of God and it was terrible,' he sobbed. 'And now I can't get it out of my head.'

17.50

'I have one question.' Simon was making minor adjustments to the walkie-talkie in an attempt to improve reception.

'Shoot.'

'I wish folk in the army wouldnae say shoot all the time,' Dave moaned. 'Do ye no' get enough o' that here?'

'Lesley's got a fake security disk and now we've got the security codes to the base,' Simon said, ignoring Dave's protests. 'But the codes change all the time and we won't be able to access those changes in the future. So how can we use this escape route twice? It's only going to work for one night.'

'Final part of the plan,' Jimmy said, taking off the headphones for the last time. 'Lesley's going to put a fake security disk in the gate console, but she's not going to punch in the code.'

'I don't get you.'

'In ten minutes I'm going to use our security access to shut down every electronic lock on the base.'

'What!'

'Only for a split second.' Jimmy held up his hands. 'They'll lock again immediately. Nobody will even notice.'

113

'What good will *that* do?'

'When the locks go off-line, Lesley will insert the fake disk in the back gate. When they come back on, that disk will automatically be part of the security system. Since it's a blank disk, *whatever* code she then punches in will work. What's more, it will always work—it'll be hard-wired into base security—unauthorized and undetected.'

'That's pure dead brilliant, man!' Dave enthused.

'We can use our *own* code anytime we want and it won't show up on any surveillance data. Our personal access to any lock, gate, computer . . . whatever.'

'I take my hat off to you,' Simon said, his normally taciturn face split by a wide grin. 'Except I don't have one, so I'll take Dave's hat off instead.' He knocked Dave's Burberry cap across the room with a well aimed swipe.

'Do that again, ya wee gadgie, an' I'll take your *head* aff.'

'This next bit has to be timed perfectly,' Jimmy said. 'When Lesley gives the signal, we shut down the locks and turn them on again—just long enough for her to stick the disk in the back gate.'

'An' you're sure this isnae gonnae backfire?'

'Pinegrove's locks will be open for a split second,' Jimmy said confidently. 'What can go wrong in a split second?'

17.55

Cowper and Cruikshank sat opposite each other in the interview room. The major tapped a large fist against his chin while Cruikshank played nervously with the lead of his iPod. The observer had been taken away and placed in confinement. Monk and Olly stood behind the security chief, looking slightly stunned.

'Let me start by saying I underestimated you, son.' Cowper managed a grudging compliment. 'Though I still don't understand what the hell just happened.' He turned to Monk and Olly. 'Gentlemen?'

'Haven't got a clue.'

Cruikshank was trembling all over. He looked balefully at the adults.

'May-Rose didn't bite any of that team, did she?'

'Not according to the observer.'

'Changing someone's genetic make-up by biting them is hard enough to accept,' the boy continued. 'I can't believe she infected them with an *airborne* gene. Besides, May-Rose didn't go mad, just the others.'

'That's true,' Olly agreed, glancing at Monk for support. The doctor looked away, still perplexed. It was a feeling he was getting used to but he certainly didn't like it.

'So we're back to the mouse,' Cruikshank continued. 'You said the creature had its DNA altered and it became smarter. Much smarter.'

'Yes.'

'And, somehow, May-Rose has the same alterations?'

'Again, yes.'

Cruikshank put his iPod on the table and stopped fidgeting.

'But May-Rose was a genius to begin with,' he said.

'Wait a minute, kid.' Comprehension began to dawn on Monk's face and he expelled a puff of derision. 'Are you saying what I think you're saying? That May-Rose has become so smart she *talked* those men into murdering each other?'

'That's what I'm saying.'

'That's ludicrous! Even if she could, why would she?'

'I don't think she wanted them to kill each other. I think she wanted them to let her out.' Cruikshank tapped the table, trying to order his thoughts. 'But the big guy, Bunton, he was stronger willed than the others. He resisted. So . . . she made the rest of the team attack him. She also tried to talk to the observer, but he smashed the intercom before he succumbed. Turned him mad in the process, though.'

'My mother-in-law could do that,' said Cowper showing an unexpected sliver of humour. But Monk was having none of it.

'Much as I admire the complexity of a child's imagination, this is sheer nonsense.'

'I don't have any imagination,' Cruikshank retorted nastily. 'I'm a scientist.'

'This *is* kind of far-fetched, kid,' Olly said.

'You know what a meme is, don't you?' Cruikshank turned to the bearded man.

'Sure,' Olly replied. 'Memes are ideas or values, passed on from person to person, group to group. Some die out, but the strongest ones become an irreversible part of human culture. Religion, music, love, they're all memes we can't imagine living without.'

'And how do we pass memes on?'

'Through language mostly,' Olly said without hesitation. 'In fact language is a meme too.'

'Suppose May-Rose has an idea so powerful it's hard to resist. And because of your meddling she's suddenly evolved into a super-intelligent being. She may have found a way to communicate an idea that's stronger than using ordinary language—a way of saying it maybe. A new kind of vocal inflection that we've never thought of, maybe even a form of hypnotism.' The boy rubbed his head in frustration. 'Suppose she wants to get out and start spreading that idea?'

'Enough,' Monk snapped. 'There's absolutely no evidence for *this* ridiculous idea.'

'Your evidence is sitting in the adjoining rooms,' Cruikshank persisted. 'A super-intelligent girl who somehow managed to talk four adults into killing each other. An observer who had no physical contact with her and no symptoms of any virus—but went mad after listening to her.'

'That leaves one question,' Major Cowper said. 'Why does she want to speak to you?'

And suddenly Cruikshank knew why.

May-Rose had been in on Jimmy Hicks's plan to get off the base tonight. Unfortunately, she had been stuck down here for two days and didn't know all the details of that plan. Only the other children did.

So she had picked one of them and asked that he be brought down to Bunker 10.

Him.

May-Rose intended to get out of that booth somehow. And she wanted Cruikshank to be near at hand when she did. Then he could provide her with details of how to get off the base entirely.

Whether he wanted to or not.

17.57

Sherman and his team sat on pallets in a grey windowless room. The woman in the white lab coat was going from one to the other dabbing their necks with an anaesthetic swab. Sherman still wasn't sure if she was a nurse, a doctor, or just some hired hand. It occurred to him that he didn't know her name, but now didn't seem the right time to ask.

'What's going on?' Nulce said, fidgeting on his pallet. 'I forget to wash behind my ears or something?'

'You'll be given a shot to knock you out,' the woman replied curtly. 'Then tiny transmitters will be implanted at the base of your skull.'

'Excuse me?' Nulce visibly winced.

'You won't feel it,' Sherman said. 'I've already had it done once. The device transmits images of the game directly into your neural network.'

'Very clever.' Darren gingerly felt the back of his head. 'You think you're in the game, but the game is actually in you.'

'I don't like the idea of someone messing around with my brain,' Nulce complained.

'That's assuming you have one.' Madrid stretched out languidly on her pallet. She didn't seem to be interested in making friends. Sherman gave her a cold look.

'All of you listen to me,' he said forcefully. 'We're a team, even if we hardly know each other. So, from this point on, we act like one.'

'For two million dollars I'd marry the broad,' Nulce said, leering at Madrid.

The door opened and the white-coated woman bumped a steel trolley into the room. On top of the shiny surface were five large syringes.

'Sleepy-time, people,' she said jovially, pulling on a pair of latex gloves. Darren's eyes almost popped out of his head when he saw the size of the needles.

'I'm going to die right away if she sticks that in me,' he moaned.

'What exactly is in the syringes?' Madrid said.

'Don't ask me, sweetie, I just give the injections and change bedpans.' The assistant depressed the plunger and a thin fountain of clear liquid squirted into the air. 'The pay's rubbish too.'

Darren groaned and lay back.

'Get it over with then.' He gave a miserable little laugh, closed his eyes and stretched out his arm. 'I don't think the colonel *wants* us to get out of this alive.'

Madrid looked across at Sherman and he saw doubt and mistrust in her eyes.

Though Darren had been joking, Sherman had the horrible feeling Madrid was thinking along the same lines.

PART 4

18.00 hours—19.00 hours

Hypnosis: A state of consciousness in which a person appears to lose all power of voluntary action or thought and to be highly responsive to suggestions and directions from the hypnotist

Oxford English Dictionary

18.00

Lesley and Barn marched up and down the perimeter fence, sweeping their flashlights around in what they hoped was a military manner, until they saw the torches of Smith and Jakar, bobbing down the guardhouse stairs and heading back towards the base. As soon as the soldiers' beams were out of sight they ran to the back gate, kicking up powdery snow in a glistening cloud. Lesley clicked on her walkie-talkie.

'Hicks?'

'Right here,' the radio crackled back. 'Over.'

'Black Mambo and Big Mongoose have reached the gate.'

'Who?'

'Me and Barn, of course.'

'Big Mongoose?' Barn contemplated his new code name. 'I like that. I think I'll get everyone to call me Big Mongoose from now on.'

'Dave and Simon have set up a digital loop on the laser cameras at the gate,' Jimmy said. 'They'll show an empty forest for the next few hours—it's lifted from the training simulation we were working on. You can pass right in front of the lens undetected.'

'Fantastic.' Lesley pulled off her gloves and fished the fake security disk from the pocket of her fleece jacket. 'I'm ready to go.'

'All right.' Tension was evident in Jimmy's voice, even over the static-ridden airwaves. 'I'm about to shut down the locks. You put the disk in the back gate and, when I turn the locks on again, that blank disk will be hardwired into the security system. Whatever number we punch through it will act as a proper code from that point on—and only *we'll* know it exists.'

'OK.'

There was a pause. Jimmy spoke again.

'Er . . . you have to tell me the number you're going to pick. Otherwise I won't be able to use it when I get there.'

'Right. Of course. It's . . . er . . . one, two, three, four.'

'That's a bit simple.'

'You got a terrible memory, Hicks. Wouldn't want you to forget it.'

There was a chuckle from the other end. 'I have to make a detour and drop Simon's formula down the well. It's wrapped in a waterproof oilskin. You get through the gate and hide in the trees. Give a shout when you see me come through.'

'Don't be all day then.' Wisps of condensation swirled around Lesley's head as she spoke. 'It's pretty cold to be sitting around in the snow.'

'I'll be speeding towards you on wings of desire.'

'Corny, Hicks, but romantic all the same. This date is starting to look promising.'

'Can't wait. Over and out.'

Lesley grinned to herself, slapping her arms to keep warm. Barn blew loudly into his hands.

'Can I go back now? I'm freezing.'

'Yeah.' Lesley gave him a hug. 'And thank you for everything.'

'You have a good time, Lesley,' Barn said. 'Don't eat any yellow snow.'

He pulled up his hood and headed back towards the buildings.

In the dormitory Jimmy glanced across at Simon and Dave. He held up the walkie-talkie so that Lesley could hear what was going on.

'Ready?'

Simon raised his head and nodded, then went back to typing on his console. 'Shutting down Pinegrove's electronic locks . . . now!'

'The disk is in, Hicks,' Lesley hissed over the walkie-talkie.

'And . . . reactivating the locks . . . ' Dave's voice followed almost immediately. 'Bingo!'

The boys sat back in unison. There was silence. No alarm bells rang. There were no running footsteps in the corridor.

'Ya dancer! Go on yersel', Hicksy man. We did it!'

'Punching in lock override code one, two, three, four and removing disk.' Lesley's walkie-talkie crackled to life. 'The gate's open, Jimmy! I'm through and punching in the same code on the other side. And . . . it's locked again.'

Her voice trembled with unsuppressed glee. 'Hicks, I'm outside Pinegrove!'

'Get to the trees and wait.' Jimmy grinned. 'I'll be there soon.'

* * *

In the lowest level of the base, one door swung slowly backwards and forwards on its well-oiled hinges. It had only been unlocked for a second— but that second was all the person inside needed. She may not have known every part of Jimmy Hicks's plan, but she knew the part about disabling the locks. After all, she had designed the disk.

It was just a matter of listening for the exact moment the lock mechanism deactivated and then giving the door a push.

May-Rose was out.

18.10

Cowper, Cruikshank, Dr Monk, and Olly were taking a short break in the interview room, sipping tea out of plastic cups and eating ginger snaps. It was more to calm their nerves than anything else.

'Suppose for a second you're right, kid,' Olly said. Monk gave a sarcastic snort, but the bearded researcher carried on. 'What the hell does May-Rose want *you* for? No offence, of course.'

'None taken.' Cruikshank wasn't about to land himself in hot water by mentioning the escape plan—or the fact that May-Rose had initially been part of it. He pretended the question had been a broader one.

'I think she's evolved into something we can't comprehend,' he said earnestly. 'She may be looking at some big picture that even my intellect can't understand.'

'Not like you to be modest, son,' Major Cowper said acerbically.

A rattling staccato sound came from somewhere far off in the corridors outside. Olly and Monk barely noticed it, but Cowper jerked out of his seat.

'That's gunfire.' He moved swiftly to the door and hammered on it. Two guards backed in, weapons already cocked.

'You hear that, Major?' one of them hissed.

Cowper didn't have to reply. The bursts were closer together now and getting louder.

'Doctor Monk. Grab your man and return to your lab,' Cowper snapped. 'You two, get this boy to the lift and take him to the surface.'

'What about you, sir?'

Cowper pulled his automatic pistol from its holster.

'I'll be along presently,' he said. Then he turned and ran down the corridor.

18.11

Jimmy Hicks shook hands with Simon and Dave and shouldered his rucksack. Inside were several Mars Bars, a bottle of wine he'd stolen from the canteen, Simon's formula for Stripped Light, and a present for Lesley wrapped in blue Christmas paper.

'When you see Barn, tell him to hurry up,' Simon reminded him. 'He's probably stopped to build a snowman or something.'

'Are the cameras guarding the outside door still rigged to show an empty corridor?' Jimmy asked.

'Naw, man. We put them back on as a practical joke.'

'Yeah, yeah. See you tomorrow,' Jimmy grinned. Then he slipped out of the dormitory.

18.13

The guards ushered Cruikshank out of the room and hurried him along the passageways.

'I left my iPod behind,' the boy said apprehensively. 'I'd just bought a matching leather case for it.'

The soldiers didn't respond. They walked silently on the balls of their feet, weapons held in front of them, eyes trained on each passing door. Cruikshank noticed with alarm that the lights on the security cameras overhead weren't blinking any more. His escorts had seen this too, one nodding briefly to the other in the direction of the ceiling. Each time they reached a bend in the corridor, one soldier would dart round, covering the new area, then beckon for his companion to follow.

Cruikshank's palms were sweating. He wondered if, somehow, Jimmy Hicks's escape plan had gone wrong and this was the cause of the alarms.

'Can't you use the intercoms or a walkie-talkie or something?' Cruikshank was feeling dizzy with fear and his legs were trembling like harp strings. 'Find out what's going on.'

'And give away our position in the process?' one guard replied without looking round. 'Until the precise nature of the danger is identified we maintain radio silence.'

'Base policy,' the other added.

After a few minutes they reached one long, dimly lit passage. At the far end Cruikshank could see the doors of a lift, their route to salvation. Then a horrible thought struck him.

'What if this unidentified danger is above us as well?' he ventured.

'Then stay behind us when we exit the lift.'

'Thanks.'

There was a burst of automatic fire behind them. One of the guards spun away from Cruikshank and hit the opposite wall, eyes opening wide in astonishment. He slid to the floor, jerking spasmodically, a bright patch of crimson spreading across his chest. The other soldier flung Cruikshank further up the corridor and crouched down, swinging his rifle round the corner. He let off a burst of automatic fire then withdrew his arm and flattened himself against the wall as return bursts gouged chips from the plaster inches from his head.

Cruikshank bounded to his feet, his whole body shaking.

'Head for the lift!' the soldier shouted. 'You need the base security code to activate it. The number is PD641 . . . ' His voice trailed off.

'What? What is it?' The terrified boy felt the hairs rise on the back of his neck. The soldier pointed and Cruikshank whirled round.

May-Rose was standing between him and the lift, flanked by five soldiers—they had stepped silently out of one of the doors dotted along the final corridor.

Cruikshank's protector swung his gun violently back, slamming the stock into his shoulder and squinting along the barrel, but the boy was directly in his line of fire.

Cruikshank's remaining guard was doomed and he knew it. The look on his face registered despair, anger, and fear in one horrific countenance. Then he shut one eye and pulled the trigger.

The soldier to the far left of May-Rose fell backwards, a fountain of blood spouting from his forehead. Cruikshank flung himself to the ground again as May-Rose's other bodyguards returned fire. His only ally evaporated in a mass of blood and bullets. Somewhere in the distance a klaxon began to wail.

The boy buried his head in his hands to block out the sight, bile rising in his throat.

May-Rose motioned to her escort. 'Go and see if the lift is still operating. Cruikshank and I have to talk.'

The men turned as one and marched towards the lift. Cruikshank tentatively raised his head and May-Rose gave him a reassuring smile.

The boy was definitely not reassured.

'We haven't got very long to get to the surface,' May-Rose said calmly. 'Any minute now the Ops Centre will panic and change the security codes that operate the lifts.' Her voice was soft and childish with only a hint of her Asian origins. 'Then we'll all be trapped down here.'

Cruikshank kept silent. He was still sprawled on

the floor, trying not to retch. There was a lump in his throat the size of a potato.

The girl raised a knowing finger. 'But Jimmy Hicks and Lesley intended to install an override code on all the security functions,' she continued. 'As part of their escape plan.'

She turned the finger and beckoned to the sprawling boy. Cruikshank got unsteadily to his feet, on legs that would hardly support him, hands held out placatingly in front.

'I don't know anything about the override code, May-Rose,' he pleaded. 'I've been down here just like you.'

'Ah well, even geniuses make mistakes.' The girl's narrow black eyes twinkled with misplaced humour. 'I imagine that Lieutenant Dunwoody and his squad have instructions to kill anybody trying to get to the surface anyway. It's called a containment contingency.'

She sighed wistfully.

'That override code would have come in very handy in the fight that's coming. 'Cause, let's face it, the only way you and I are getting off this base alive is to outwit Dunwoody's men or kill them.'

The soldiers reached the lifts and one of them punched in the code. A whirr of cables indicated that the lift was descending. They stood back, not talking, not looking at each other.

'What have you done to these men?' the boy whispered.

'They're under my protection and guidance now.' May-Rose smiled in their direction. 'The human race has strayed, Cruikshank, and I will gather or lay waste to those I meet—depending on whether or not they give me trouble.'

She gave an impish grin that made Cruikshank's flesh creep.

'I'm here to save humanity from its sins.'

18.14

'Simon. You want tae come an' take a look at this.' Diddy Dave was bent over his computer. 'There's something awfy funny goin' on with the systems on the lower levels.'

'Are you still hacking into base security?' Simon scowled. 'That's asking for trouble.'

'Ahm jist havin' a wee nosey.'

'What do you mean, funny? What kind of funny? Is this because of something we did?'

'If it wuz, we better get packin' now.' Dave rubbed his greasy hair. 'Communications are down and alarms are goin' off all over the base.'

'Dammit. I knew Jimmy's plan would backfire!' Simon snarled.

'Ah think we'd better find oot exactly what's happening,' Dave said, tapping at keys. 'Jimmy's transmitters are powerful enough to reach the Ops Centre, an' they work as receivers too. Let's see if we can pick up signals from in there.'

'Are you crazy?'

The door of the dormitory burst open and Barn ran in. The other two almost fell off their seats. The larger boy stopped and began slapping snow from his legs.

'Were you born in a barn, Barn! Ever hear of knocking?'

'What's going on, guys?' Barn was bent double, breathing heavily. His face was an alarming shade of purple. 'There's sirens hooting all over the place.'

Simon bit his lip.

'All right, Dave. Tap into the Operations Room. See what kind of mess we've made.'

'Aye, aye, Captain,' Dave replied. Despite his joking, sweat was standing out on his white forehead.

'Ah just hope there's somethin' we can dae tae fix it.'

18.15

There was a ping as the lift reached the lower floor. May-Rose's escorts stepped back and pointed their weapons at the door. As it slid open a metal canister was flung out, landing between their feet.

'Grenade!' One man roared and May-Rose's soldiers flung themselves away from the cylinder, landing on the floor and curling into balls to minimize the impact of the blast on their bodies.

Major Cowper stepped out of the lift, rifle in hand.

'Actually it's a tin of spray paint,' he said. 'Thought I'd taught you better than that.'

Then he opened fire. The men on the floor were dead in seconds.

May-Rose turned and faced him.

'You don't want to kill me, Major,' she said loudly. 'I'm your salvation.'

Her voice had changed. Cruikshank couldn't say how, but it definitely wasn't the same person talking. There was something so commanding in her tone that he couldn't imagine anyone disobeying her.

Cowper seemed unfazed. He tossed the empty rifle into the lift and drew his pistol. Then he advanced down the corridor towards the children—the gun clenched, execution style, in both hands.

For the first time Cruikshank noticed that the Chief of Security had white wires coming from his ears. A tinny sound accompanied the major as he approached.

'Stop right there, Major Cowper,' May-Rose commanded, even louder.

'Can't hear you, I'm afraid,' Cowper shouted. He raised his weapon and pointed it at the girl.

'He's wearing my iPod!' Cruikshank stammered.

May-Rose clenched her fists in fury. Cruikshank could almost feel her massive mental processes looking for a way to overcome this hurdle.

'Cruikshank, get into the lift and take it to the surface,' Cowper yelled. The boy glanced at May-Rose then began to edge past her towards the major.

'Stay where you are,' May-Rose hissed.

Cruikshank stopped dead, as if he had been slapped in the face. Though he strained every muscle to move, his legs refused to take him any further. He tried to will himself forward. It was no use.

Cowper strode forwards, grabbed Cruikshank by his blond hair and pulled him roughly along the corridor. His gun was still trained on May-Rose.

'Get going!' he yelled at the boy.

Tears welled up in Cruikshank's eyes.

'I *can't*,' he pleaded in a small voice.

'You're not going anywhere,' May-Rose said in her terrible commanding tone. Major Cowper's face darkened. He swung his gun and pointed it at Cruikshank.

'Wait a minute! It's not my fault!' the boy screamed.

Major Cowper fired. The bullet whizzed past, inches from Cruikshank's head. He felt a burning sensation near his temple and a loud ringing filled his ears, momentarily deafening him.

'Go!' Cowper shouted. He lowered his gun and fired again. The floor between the boy's feet exploded and splinters of wood and hot metal from the ricochet embedded themselves in the flesh of his legs. With a howl of pain the boy turned and ran. Major Cowper kept firing and Cruikshank saw gouges appear in the floor beside him as he raced towards the lift.

'Come back, Cruikshank!' May-Rose screamed. 'Cowper will kill me!' Her voice rose in pitch and volume till it finally drowned out the ringing in his ears.

'YOU COME BACK! COME BACK AND SAVE ME!'

The words were like molten metal, burning inside his head. He barrelled into the lift and hit the far wall, clutching at his temples.

Major Cowper was still facing him, headphones on his head and a satisfied smirk on his face.

Cruikshank gasped in horror.

Behind the Security Chief another group of soldiers had appeared. May-Rose gestured angrily and the men moved towards the major. With music blaring into his ears, Cowper couldn't hear them approaching.

'Behind you!' Cruikshank screamed waving his arms. 'Look behind you!'

'What?' Cowper frowned. Then his eyes widened, as he realized what the boy was trying to convey.

One of the soldiers opened fire.

Cowper sank to his knees with a cry, arms outstretched in a futile attempt to slow the troops pushing past him towards the lift. Cruikshank reached up and punched the button for the surface.

As the doors slid together he caught sight of the major for the last time, lying face down on the floor. The lift shuddered and began to ascend.

The boy sank to the floor, weeping hysterically.

18.16

The Operations Room on level one was in chaos. Commander Saunders and Lieutenant Dunwoody were shouting orders to the technicians and alarm lights were ringing on every console.

'Status report!' the commander yelled. 'What the hell is happening in the lower levels?'

'It . . . seems to be some sort of mutiny, sir,' Warrant Officer Took stammered in disbelief. 'We've monitored our own men breaking the security cameras down there. There's gunfire, too, but we can't get a coherent report because all the intercom systems are offline below level two. Looks like they've been sabotaged too.'

'What in God's name is causing this?'

'Before the cameras went down we spotted the girl, May-Rose, in a corridor of the lowest level.'

'She's out?'

Took hesitated. 'She appears to be in charge of the rebels, sir.'

'Change all security codes right now!' Commander Saunders bellowed. 'We have to keep her trapped down there.'

'I'm on it, sir.'

'This has got to be the result of some virus.' Dunwoody looked up. He had a radio in his hand that he had been speaking into. 'There *must* be a contamination down there driving your men mad.'

'Are *your* soldiers ready, Lieutenant?' the commander snapped.

'With the codes changed, nobody down there will be able to use the lifts any more, so I'll deploy my men to cover the stairs—they're the only exits left.'

Dunwoody pulled himself upright. 'And I'm formally requesting that you put *your* remaining military personnel under my command during this period. Those that are still obeying your orders,' he added pointedly.

The commander swallowed hard.

'Agreed,' he said finally, motioning to Took. 'Raise all the troops you can. Place them under Dunwoody's command.'

'Will do, sir.'

The lieutenant took the commander gently aside.

'My men can stop people getting out but we can't stop a virus spreading,' he whispered. 'What's the protocol in the event of a contagious leak in Bunker Ten?'

The commander noted Dunwoody's use of the nickname. The lieutenant was a fast learner.

'We seal off the lowest level with vacuum doors. The air pressure in the bottom of the base is kept at less than the surface. Air flows downwards, keeping any airborne virus from spreading.' He spread his own hands in exasperation. 'But we don't know if this *is* a virus. We don't know *what* we're dealing with.'

'We need to get in touch with High Command. Let them know what's going on.'

'Yes. That's right.' The commander was blinking rapidly, rubbing one hand up and down the side of his leg. 'They have to be told.'

'Then what are we waiting for?' Dunwoody snarled. 'Things to get *worse*?'

The commander swallowed again. 'Open a link to HQ,' he said.

'Yes, sir.' Took was about to obey when he gave a start.

'Someone's trying to communicate with us from Bunker Ten,' he said in astonishment. 'On the intercom system.'

'Patch him in on the loudspeaker.'

A cracked, pain-filled voice suddenly filled the Ops Room. 'This is Oliver Torrence . . . Olly . . . from Project Flower . . . I haven't got long.'

'Where are you, Olly?' the commander said loudly.

'He can't hear you, sir,' Took interrupted. 'It's a one-way communication.'

But Olly was ahead of them. 'I've barricaded myself in Bunker Ten,' the voice said. 'But I've been shot. Badly I think . . . ' There was a burst of wet coughing and a low groan. 'You have to listen to me,' Olly continued. 'I know what you're thinking, but there is no airborne virus down here, do you understand? This contagion can only be transmitted through close physical contact.' There was another violent bout of coughing. The commander looked down and ran a hand over his face.

Olly gave a ragged intake of breath. It was drowned out by a hammering sound.

'Someone's trying to break into the lab to reach that man,' Dunwoody said.

'I repeat. There is no danger from a virus!' Olly's voice was weaker now and slightly slurred. 'It's May-Rose.'

'How? Explain yourself,' the commander urged, forgetting that Olly couldn't hear him. But the injured man was getting to that.

'May-Rose can control others simply by talking to them. Don't ask me how, but she can!'

A rasping whine spun into life, as if someone had turned on a power tool.

'I disabled the lower intercom systems except the outlet I'm patched into, but it won't take her long to get them working again. You have to shut them down entirely. And for God's sake destroy any means of communication with the outside world.'

Olly rallied himself for one final plea.

'If May-Rose can transmit off the base, she'll be able to control anyone she reaches. I'm begging you, Commander.'

The whine had reached an unbearable pitch, as nerve shredding as nails across a blackboard.

'They're almost in!' Olly cried.

'I think we should do what he says,' Dunwoody urged. 'Just in case.'

Saunders was rigid as a stick of ice, his jaw working silently.

'But there's something you don't know about Pinegrove,' he whispered. 'There's a secret security system that is activated when . . . '

'Commander!' Olly shouted above the shuddering drone. 'May-Rose has power beyond our imagination. Don't let her out! Don't let her talk to the outside world!'

There was a loud bang and then silence.

'What do you think?' Dunwoody urged.

'I *can't* authorize cutting communication to headquarters—certainly not without the backing of my Security Chief,' the commander fumed. He grabbed Took by the shoulder. 'You sure you can't raise Major Cowper?'

'Sorry, sir.'

Took looked startled.

'Wait a minute. There's a *visual* communication coming in.'

'Put it through.'

Major Cowper appeared on the screen above their head.

'Sorry, sir, I haven't had much of a chance to call in.' Cowper put a finger to his lips. 'There are a lot of crazies with guns running around.'

'Do you know the situation?'

'Affirmative, sir.'

'Do you think that we should isolate Pinegrove from outside communication?'

There was a pause. Major Cowper narrowed his eyes. Then he spoke.

'I do, sir. Most strongly.'

'Warrant Officer Took, disable all communication links with the base. That includes HQ.' The commander slammed his fist against his leg.

'Disable them permanently. Authorization code two, four ABD.'

'This is confirmed by Major Cowper. Authorization code one, two, three, four.'

'One, two, three, four?' The commander looked hesitant. 'That isn't a proper code.'

'But it's working, sir!' Took interrupted, tapping his keyboard. 'Our lines to the outside are shorting. Only the internal communication system is still operable. Well . . . partially.'

'I have to go, sir,' Cowper whispered, looking off-screen to something on his right. 'Not very safe to stay in one place. I'll report when I can.'

'Wait a minute . . . ' the commander began, but the screen went blank.

In the dormitory, Simon removed the headset and microphone. On the screen in front of him, the virtual Major Cowper was frozen in mid-goodbye. Simon's hands were shaking so badly he could hardly tap the keys.

'Did I do OK?'

'Ye fooled them, man. Gave it the full bhoona. Let's just hope we're doin' the right thing, eh?' Dave ran nervous fingers through his sweaty hair and held up the walkie-talkie. 'Ye werenae so smart wi' the radio though. Ye left it switched on an' the cell's gone dead. I cannae get in touch wi' Hicksy or Lesley.'

Simon grimaced in apology.

'Damn! We need to get them back here before

they get shot as terrorists or something,' he said. 'Barn?'

'Yeah.' The large boy was standing upright now, though his face was still an alarming shade of red.

'Jimmy must be at the old well by now. I need you to go get him and bring him back.'

Barn's large features crumpled.

'C'mon, big man,' Dave cajoled. 'You could do wi' the exercise.'

'OK! Big Mongoose to the rescue,' Barn wheezed and vanished out of the door again.

'Are we still overriding the cameras at exit four, so he can get out?'

'Aye, we are.' Dave brought up the base schematics. 'They're so busy fighting each other in the complex that they're no' paying much attention to the outlying buildings—there's naebody but us in them anyway. Even the guards took off for the main buildings as soon as the alarms went off.'

'Dave?'

'Aye?'

'Is there a way to reroute the sound from the intercoms in this building, so they go through our computer instead of the speakers?'

'Nae problem. It's a digital system.'

'And use voice decoding software to convert the sounds into text that we can read?'

'Nae sweat, Si.' Dave looked puzzled. 'Why?'

'If May-Rose starts using the intercom system, I think it'd be better if we could read what she's saying, rather than hear it. You agree?'

'I'm on it.' Dave grinned at his spectacled friend. 'You'd make a good officer, man.'

Simon gave a grimace.

'I've decided to quit the army if we live through this.'

18.17

Barn reached the outer door, panting with exertion. Klaxons were still sounding below and now he could hear shouted voices. His head was hurting and he was frightened and confused. In his mind he went over calculations in a vain attempt to stay calm.

'111,111,111 times 111,111,111 equals 12,345, 678,987,654,321,' he chanted, nodding his head violently. He punched 1234 into the door console and pushed it open. A blast of freezing night air blew across his face and he breathed in a deep lungful of dark, clean air.

A figure stepped from the shadows further down the corridor. Barn whimpered and pressed himself against the wall, eyes tightly shut.

'What the hell are you *doing*?'

The voice was instantly recognizable. Barn opened one eye.

Cruikshank was standing in front of him, lab coat splattered with blood. He was holding Major Cowper's automatic rifle awkwardly against his chest.

'I've been sent to fetch Jimmy Hicks back,' Barn rasped. 'He's out near the old well. Something has gone awfully wrong.'

'Don't I know it.' Cruikshank moved to the door

and looked cautiously into the night. There was no sound from outside. 'Why is he at the well? He's supposed to be meeting Lesley outside the perimeter.'

'He's going to hide Simon's time travel formula first.' Barn glanced nervously round. 'So we have a copy somewhere safe.'

'Smart move.' Cruikshank nodded approvingly. 'Listen, you go back upstairs to the dormitory. I'll get Jimmy.'

Barn looked uncertain. 'Dave and Simon sent *me*,' he said hesitantly.

'They did. But I know exactly what's going on,' Cruikshank insisted. 'I can explain everything to Jimmy on the way back. What's the override code, so I can get back in?'

'One, two, three, four.'

'Fine. Tell Dave and Simon that Major Cowper is dead.'

Barn's eyes widened. He gave a gulp and peeled off his thermal jacket.

'Take my coat then. It's freezing out there.'

The jacket fitted easily over Cruikshank's lab coat and almost reached his knees. The boy fumbled awkwardly at the zip.

'My hands are shaking too much to do it up.'

Barn knelt and fastened the zipper for him. Then he ruffled his companion's hair and ran back the way he had come.

Cruikshank watched until he had vanished round the corner. With a grimace, he hefted the rifle onto his shoulder and limped out into the darkness.

18.20

The intercom was still silent. The staff in the Ops Room glanced nervously at each other.

Lieutenant Dunwoody was the first to react.

'I think we should disable internal communications as well as external ones,' he said. 'If this man, Olly, is telling the truth, we don't want May-Rose transmitting to the whole base.'

'Yes, but I've been thinking.' Commander Saunders's face was sickly white. 'What if Olly is actually on May-Rose's side? Suppose this whole "voice" thing is a ruse?' He wiped sweat from his forehead with the back of his sleeve. 'Now we've cut ourselves off from outside help. If we disable internal communications she can exploit the confusion and break out that much easier.'

'My men have their own walkie-talkies and they're on a separate system.' Dunwoody tapped a small radio attached to his belt. 'I can talk to them directly and make sure they keep the situation contained.'

'You sure?'

'This is what I do.'

The commander nodded.

'Make it so, Mr Took.' Saunders was a big fan of *Star Trek*, and had always wanted to say that. Plus he had the dreadful premonition that it might be his last chance.

Took began tapping furiously at his console, shutting down systems one by one.

'Listen, Lieutenant,' the commander began, 'I was trying to tell you earlier, there's something you don't know about Pinegrove. It has a built-in security failsafe in case of . . .'

A child's voice, soft and lilting, suddenly drifted through the Ops Room.

'This is May-Rose. I'm afraid Olly is dead.'

There was a hushed silence as everyone turned and looked at the speaker on the wall.

'But I'm not the enemy, I promise,' the girl continued. 'You listened to Olly, so you can at least listen to me.'

'Took, switch off those speakers right now!' Dunwoody shouted. But Took hesitated, his hand hovering over the transmission switch.

'Listen to me. We've made a wonderful discovery down here,' May-Rose carried on. 'And we want to share it with everyone. But Lieutenant Dunwoody and his men have been sent to prevent that. They're here to kill you all.'

'Shut down that communication!' Dunwoody commanded, his voice as stern and official as he could make it. 'That is a direct order, soldier!'

Firm as it was, Dunwoody's tone was nowhere near as imposing as the child's voice wafting across the room. Heads were beginning to turn in the lieutenant's direction. Looks that were a horrific mixture of blankness and hostility.

'Dunwoody and his men are the enemy,' the intercom whispered seductively. 'You must destroy them and set us free. You must kill them. Kill them all and let us share our discovery with you.'

The lieutenant and his men had been trained in a way the base personnel could not even imagine. They knew how to withstand the severest interrogation, to shut their minds and bodies from external pressures, to withdraw into a secret part of themselves.

Dunwoody narrowed his eyes and tuned May-Rose out—though it was harder than he could ever have believed. With a snarl he unleashed a burst from his automatic rifle into the console where Took was seated. The operator fell backwards, warding off a shower of sparks with his arms. May-Rose's voice was cut off in mid sentence.

Took struggled to his feet, fury etched across his face. Other technicians were rising from their consoles, turning towards Dunwoody with the same look. A few took tentative steps towards him.

'This is what Olly was talking about!' he shouted. 'Commander Saunders, order your men to stand down *right now*!'

But the commander also had an angry, faraway look. With trembling hands he slowly unholstered his sidearm—he seemed to be fighting against some horrible, overpowering urge he couldn't control. Biting his lip he swung the pistol towards Dunwoody.

The lieutenant had been trained in much more

than interrogation techniques. He had been trained to survive and to kill.

Without a blink he opened fire, cutting down the commander and Took where they stood. Howling their fury, the rest of the Ops Room rose from their seats and surged towards the lieutenant, some peeling off to reach the gun rack on the far wall.

Dunwoody took up a combat stance, legs apart.

He raised the weapon to his shoulder and began shooting.

18.21

Jimmy Hicks had reached the well. He rummaged around inside his parka and brought out Simon's formula, wrapped in tin foil and packed in a sandwich bag. As he raised his hand to throw it into the dark hole he heard a click behind him.

Cruikshank was standing a few feet away, pointing a rifle.

'Hand over the formula, Hicks.'

Jimmy tried to keep calm. In truth, he was as surprised as he was afraid.

'Don't be stupid, Cruikshank,' he said quietly. 'You'll never get away with this.'

'I think I will. But *your* escape plan has gone badly wrong.'

Jimmy looked sourly at the weapon. 'I can see that myself.'

'That's not what I mean.' Cruikshank jerked his head in the direction he had come. 'People are dying back there.'

As if on cue, they heard the put-put of a machine gun from the direction of the base. Jimmy's eyes widened.

'Lesley is safe outside, I take it.' Cruikshank didn't even look in the direction of the gunfire. 'But I wouldn't hold out much hope for the rest of your pals.' He motioned with the gun again. 'I'm taking the formula and getting out. You're welcome to follow . . . after a decent amount of time. Now drop the damned bag.'

'You won't shoot me.'

'You think not? Hicks, you'll just be another dead body. I've seen plenty in the last half hour.'

Despite his feigned nonchalance, Cruikshank was obviously fighting to control his emotions. His breath was coming in short sibilant bursts and he looked ready to snap. He gave an angry jerk with the gun.

Jimmy reluctantly dropped the bag and stepped back. The boy limped over and picked it up.

'I need ten minutes to get clear then you can make your choice. Get out or go back, it's all the same to me.'

'You harm Lesley and I'll kill you.'

'I have no interest in Lesley. If I see her, I'll tell her to run and never stop.' The boy was still backing away, still keeping the gun trained on Jimmy. 'After what I've just seen I don't think the army will let any of us live. Trust me.'

More gunfire drifted across the snowy waste behind them.

'I'm sorry, Jimmy,' Cruikshank said abruptly.

It was the first time he had ever called Jimmy Hicks by his first name.

Then he turned and limped towards the rear gate.

18.25

Lieutenant Dunwoody staggered from the Ops Room and into the corridor. He was soaked with blood, wide white eyes staring from a mask of crimson. One arm hung limply by his side but most of the gore covering him came from the people he had just cut down. He sank to the floor, pulled the walkie-talkie from his belt and opened a channel to his team.

'This is Dunwoody,' he croaked. 'I haven't got time to explain but all personnel at Pinegrove base must now be treated as hostile. I mean *all* of them.' He stopped, looking in horror at the red rivulets dripping from his hands. 'Everyone on this installation who is not part of my team are to be terminated with extreme prejudice. Do I make myself clear?'

There was a crackle from the radio as his sergeant came on the air.

'Say again, sir?'

'You heard me,' Dunwoody replied furiously. 'You shoot anyone you meet on sight. Anyone not on our team. Men. Women. Children. Is that understood?'

There was silence on the other end.

'I said, is that understood!?'

'Understood, sir. Sir?'

'Yes, Sergeant?'

'What was going on with that message on the intercom? It made me feel very . . . strange.'

Dunwoody pressed his bloody fists against his forehead. Then he spoke into the walkie-talkie again.

'You OK?'

'As far as I know we all are.'

'Then secure the upper levels. Once you've done that, lead a small team to the surface and disable all the base vehicles.' He hesitated for a second. 'Disable our vehicles too. And search the surface buildings. Terminate anyone you encounter.'

'There are only a group of kids up there.'

Dunwoody was relentless. 'It's a child who caused this, Sergeant.'

There was silence again. Finally his subordinate spoke.

'I'll get it done, sir. Over and out.'

18.30

'Dave, Simon. Are you there? Come in. It's Jimmy!'

There was no answer from the walkie-talkie in his hand. Jimmy sat on the ground, Cruikshank's words chasing each other round and round in his head.

—Lesley is safe outside.

He looked towards the woods and the fence and freedom.

—But I wouldn't hold out much hope for the rest of your pals.

There was almost constant gunfire coming from the direction of the base. Jimmy slammed a fist into the snow, then picked up the walkie-talkie again.

'Dammit! Dave! Simon! It's Jimmy. Are you there? Come in! It's Jimmy.'

Just outside the perimeter fence, Lesley crouched on an old oilskin and peered over a clump of gorse. She heard the sound of breaking branches and ducked down behind the bush, giggling to herself.

Jimmy was coming. Tonight was *the* night. It was going to be great!

A lone form lurched out of the darkness and

into the clearing. Lesley knew immediately that it wasn't Jimmy Hicks. It was too short and the walk was wrong—in fact the stranger seemed to be limping.

The moon came out from behind a cloud and Lesley gasped.

It was Cruikshank. And he was carrying a rifle.

The girl crouched down further and peeped through a gap in the jagged scrub. The blond boy stopped and removed Barn's jacket, revealing a bloodstained lab coat underneath. Tearing it off, he threw it away with an angry grunt. It drifted down and blended into the snow, invisible except for splatters of red down the front.

Cruikshank looked at the gun in disgust, then flung that away too. He put the jacket back on, shambled across the clearing and vanished into the trees, heading away from Pinegrove.

Lesley waited until he was out of earshot before picking up her walkie-talkie.

'Hicks,' she whispered. 'You there?'

'I'm here.' Jimmy's voice sounded strained and tearful.

'What the hell's going on? I just saw Cruikshank! He had a gun but he threw it away. Where are *you*?' The girl's frightened sentences came tumbling out on top of each other.

'Lesley, you have to go after him. He's stolen Simon's formula.'

'The little . . . ' Lesley stopped mid-sentence. 'What about you? Aren't you coming to help me?'

There was silence from the other end.

'Hicks? What's gone wrong?'

'I have to go back.' Jimmy's voice was thick with apprehension and sorrow. 'Something terrible is happening at Pinegrove.'

'*What*, for God's sake?'

'I don't know, but I think Simon, Dave, and Barn are in danger.'

Lesley got to her feet, shaking snow from her clothes.

'Hang on. I'm coming back.'

'*No!*' Jimmy shouted. 'You can't do that! Not under any circumstances! I'll sort this out. You shadow Cruikshank. We have to know where he goes.'

'How will I reach you? The radio range is only a few hundred yards.'

'You're a genius. You'll figure out a way.'

'Are you trying to send me to safety, Hicks?'

'Nah.' She could almost see the boy's lopsided smile. 'I just don't need you getting under my feet when I'm saving everyone's arse.'

'That's very noble,' Lesley whispered. 'But I *can't* leave you.'

'Lesley, I'm begging you. I *need* you to be safe.' There was another silence. A long one this time. When Jimmy finally spoke again, his voice was calm and clear.

'I love you.'

Lesley closed her eyes and a tear slid under her dark lashes.

'Of course you do, Hicks. I'm great.'

'Over and out, Lesley. Be safe.'

The walkie-talkie went dead.

Lesley ran out into the centre of the clearing. The rifle was sticking out of the snow like a piece of battlefield debris. She snapped open the breech, the way her father had taught her, and checked the magazine.

'What? Damn thing's out of ammo.'

Dropping the gun, she pulled the flashlight from her pocket and followed Cruikshank's tracks out of the clearing and into a winding path through the forest.

18.35

Lesley had barely vanished from sight when the air in the centre of the clearing began to shimmer. A few seconds later Sherman, Madrid, Darren, and Nulce were standing in the snow. They wore dark combat gear and Sherman had on his lucky black leather jacket.

'Great.' He glanced around at the winter landscape. 'We stick out like a bunch of exclamation marks on a sheet of white paper.'

Madrid and Nulce crouched low, weapons at the ready, scanning the forest edge for any sign of hostility. Darren bent down and picked up an object by his feet.

'It's a lab coat,' he said. 'A very small lab coat with blood down the front.'

'Yeah, yeah.' Sherman took out a compass. 'So, keep your eyes open for a dwarf with a nosebleed.' He flicked the lid open and studied the needle.

'The perimeter fence is this way,' he said. 'Code for the gate is one, two, three, four. On the way to the main complex we detour to leave a strongbox at the old well.'

He motioned forward with two fingers—a move he'd copied from half a dozen war films.

'Let's head out.'

18.40

Jimmy burst into the dormitory, his hair plastered to his forehead.

'What the hell is going on?' he shouted, wild eyed. 'There's gunfire coming from the main complex.'

Barn looked behind the boy into the empty corridor.

'Where's Cruikshank?'

'Halfway up the nearest mountain, by now. And he's got the time-travel formula.'

'Jimmy!' Simon's head shot up.

'He pulled a gun on me! But he's ditched it now and Lesley's following him.' Jimmy held up his hands in a vain attempt to placate the horrified boy. 'Let's sort out the problem here first.'

'This problem's no' sortable, Hicksy. You better sit doon.'

Jimmy's expression hardened as the boys explained what had been going on. When they were finished he sat with his hands on his knees, staring into space.

'What's the situation now?' he asked suddenly.

'Most of the base personnel will have heard May-Rose over the intercom,' Simon said. 'I imagine they're under her control and trying to break her out.'

'We werenae affected because we wir just reading what she said.' Dave pointed to the transcript on the computer screen. 'And the team that arrived this morning dinnae seem to be falling for her shtick either.'

Jimmy thought about that. 'It's understandable. If they're a Special Ops force they'll be trained to withstand hypnosis and mind-altering techniques.'

'They're trying to keep everyone contained in the lower levels—maistly by shooting anything that moves.'

'I take it base communications are down now?'

'Yeah,' Simon confirmed. 'Their lieutenant, some guy called Dunwoody, finally wrecked the system—and he killed everyone in the Ops Room doing it.'

'So who's winning?' Barn asked.

'Dunwoody's SWAT team are well outnumbered, but they've got better weapons and they're obviously trained killers. I'd say it was a tie so far.'

The children looked at each other. Barn spoke up again.

'What'll we *do*?'

'I say we gie this argy-bargy a body swerve. Get oot while we can, man,' Dave said. 'Barnsy, see if you can spot anything moving oot there.'

Barn lumbered over to the dark window and peered out, shielding his eyes with his hands to block out the reflections of the worried group behind him.

Jimmy stood up.

'What about May-Rose?' he said awkwardly. 'We can't just leave her down there.'

'Are you kiddin', man?' Dave held up his hands in despair. 'She's no' exactly battin' fur the hame team any more, know?'

'Let's get out, Jimmy,' Simon agreed. 'Otherwise we're going to end up dead.'

'All right. Get what you can carry that's important to you.' Jimmy sat down at the computer. 'I'll print off another copy of your formula, Simon, and then try and delete anything that links us to this nightmare. Wait a minute . . .'

He sat back, puzzled.

'What's wrong now?' The boys gathered round.

'A *new* security program has just activated itself.' Jimmy pointed to the screen. 'It's completely separate from the existing system.'

'Let me see if I can open it.' Simon nudged Jimmy aside and began to type. 'It's not part of the mainframe, but I should at least be able to read what it does.'

A thick block of data appeared on the screen and Simon swallowed hard.

'I wish I wasn't seeing this,' he whispered. 'Pinegrove base has an automatic failsafe system in the event of a viral outbreak.'

'But we dinnae have a viral outbreak! We've got a wee lassie with a big mooth who's gone raj!'

'The system override doesn't know that.' Jimmy's eyes flicked from side to side, taking in the information. 'Fifteen minutes after any alarms go off this hidden security program kicks in. The

166

perimeter lasers turn and point inwards—reprogramming themselves automatically to fire at anything going near the fence. It's designed to stop anyone infected getting out.'

Simon looked at his watch. 'It's coming up for that fifteen minutes now,' he said in a shocked whisper.

Jimmy was clutching the sides of the console so hard, his knuckles were like white marbles. 'If no all-clear is given within half an hour, the system assumes that the infection is out of control and a countdown begins. It can only be countermanded by High Command or by Commander Saunders and Major Cowper together.'

'Countdown tae what, or do I no' want tae ken?'

'A countdown till the base self-destructs,' Jimmy said.

'But the commander and Cowper are dead and all links to Central Command are permanently frazzled.' Simon's eyes were like saucers. 'How long before this place goes *up*?'

Jimmy bit his lip. 'An hour and twenty minutes.'

'Away tae buggery! Ahm offski, man.'

'Can't we shut it down?' Simon urged. 'We've got access to the security systems.'

'No. No. This one operates independently. There's no way.'

'Dave's right then. Let's take our chances with the perimeter fence.' Simon was already on his feet and heading for his locker. 'We've got a combined IQ higher than the national debt. Surely we can beat a few lasers.'

'This is not a case where brains will overcome brawn,' Jimmy said without a trace of doubt. 'What do you think you're going to do? Talk your way past them?'

'You got any better ideas?'

Jimmy thought carefully. 'Not a one. Let's get the hell out of here.'

'Guys.' Barn had his forehead pressed against the window. 'Half a dozen of those soldiers in black are heading our way.'

'How far?'

'They're at the front door now.'

'Aw! Thanks fur the timely heid's up, flash.'

'Switch on the cameras in the corridors below and use our code to lock the outer door.' Jimmy grabbed the nearest bed and began pulling it across the floor. 'Barricade the dorm door too. Tables, lockers . . . anything heavy you can find.'

Barn lumbered over, picked up a table and computer with one mighty heave and staggered towards the door.

'What do they want, Jimmy?'

'If they're Dunwoody's men, I'm pretty sure they're coming to kill us.'

18.45

Private Kruger zigzagged behind the sergeant across the compound and up to the entrance of the West Wing. Lights on top of the building illuminated all the paths so the men hugged the walls, staying in the shadows.

'The outlying buildings are empty. Thank God it's Christmas Eve and there is minimal staff on the base.' The sergeant waved his arm and half a dozen soldiers emerged from the gloom at a run, crunching across the hardening snow and flattening themselves beside their leader. 'But there are a bunch of kids in a dormitory at the top of this block.'

'They can't actually be infected, Sarge,' Kruger said tentatively. 'Not if they've been up there while all this is going on.'

'It's not our call to make, soldier,' the sergeant retorted. 'Besides, they might have heard the girl's intercom message same as the rest of the base. We have to assume they're hostile and act accordingly.'

'Yes, sir.' Private Kruger planted a small charge against the outer door and leapt back. There was a dull thunk and a puff of smoke from the lock. He stepped forward and kicked hard. The door swung open and the men entered, rifles held in front of them.

'Hall is clear!'

The sergeant motioned again and the soldiers began climbing the stairs.

Dave watched the assailants' progress on the computer monitor.

'Don't take a flaky, guys, but you're never gonnae get a barricade built before these gadgies reach us, know?'

'Maybe we would if you'd get off your skinny butt and help.'

'Ahm no wantin' tae get ma togs dirty.'

'Aren't there any weapons in the West Wing?' Barn asked plaintively.

'No. But maybe we can make something?' Simon turned to Jimmy in desperation. 'A Molotov cocktail or some kind of bomb made out of chemicals? Hey! Can we tie bed sheets together and lower ourselves out of the window?'

Jimmy looked at the screen over Dave's shoulder.

'Not in the two minutes it'll take them to reach this floor.' He picked up his baseball bat and patted it against his hand. 'We can either hide or fight but I don't think either will do us much good.'

'If it's a square-go they're wantin', they'll be getting a Glasgow kiss fae yours truly.' Dave reversed his baseball cap so the peak was at the back and pulled a small knife from his pocket. 'And a good chibbin' an all.'

'God, there's another four of them coming in

the front door.' Simon pointed to the computer screen. 'They're catching up fast.'

Gunfire erupted from the floor below.

Simon's jaw dropped. 'The second group have opened fire on the first!'

The others crowded round the screen and watched in amazement.

Private Kruger turned at the top of the stairs in time to see his sergeant topple backwards, one bloody hand scrabbling at his chest. On either side, his companions convulsed, bobbing like marionettes, caught in a storm of bullets.

His last sight was of four strangers, one of them a woman, swinging the barrels of their weapons towards him.

Trespassers will incur the severest penalty, he thought, as the group below opened fire.

The children stood in a cluster as the door to the dormitory was forced open. Three men and a woman entered, guns in their hands. Jimmy lifted his baseball bat in a defiant gesture. Dave gave Barn a nudge.

'You better stand in front of me, big man.'

'I'm slow, Dave. Not stupid.'

'You can put your weapons down, boys.' A stocky man in a leather jacket stepped forward, lowering his gun. 'We're not going to harm you.'

He gestured to the other three and they too lowered their arms.

'My name's Sherman,' the stranger said. 'And I need your help.'

18.50

'Are you terrorists?' Barn was as straightforward as ever. Jimmy winced.

'We're not.' Sherman smiled. His expression seemed sincere. 'We're on a special mission.'

'Yer maw! You just killed the guys that were on a special mission.' Dave still held the knife in his hand. 'Whit? You on a *special*, special mission?'

Sherman's smile flickered. Madrid stepped in front of him. 'I'm an operative working for British Army Counter Intelligence,' she said. 'You don't need to be told that the situation on this base has turned into a bit of a mess.'

'You can say that again, doll.' Dave cocked his head to one side. 'You here tae fix it?'

'We are.'

'How did you get here so fast?' Realizing he wasn't about to die, Simon's natural curiosity kicked in. 'This base is in the middle of nowhere.'

'That's classified,' Nulce broke in sharply. Sherman held up his hand for silence.

'Boys. We don't have time to sit around chewing the fat. We've got a limited window to complete our mission. We've got to get down to the lowest level of Pinegrove and retrieve sensitive data. If you help us, we'll take you with us when we leave.'

'Shouldn't that be *if* you leave?' Jimmy said.

Nulce narrowed his eyes. 'What do you mean by that?'

'Half the base is trying to kill the other half. There's a genius in the basement who's probably turned Bunker Ten into a fortress. The perimeter lasers will shoot anyone who gets near the fence and the whole place is set to blow up in just over an hour.' Jimmy lowered his baseball bat. 'There are four of you. Sorry, but I don't rate your chances.'

'Then it's a pity we're all you've got,' Sherman replied pleasantly.

'We have the element of surprise,' Madrid joined in. 'We have the latest technology, better than the most advanced stuff here. And if you help, we have four geniuses who've tapped into base security and can get us anywhere undetected.'

The boys looked astonished.

'How could you know that?'

Nulce smirked 'You'd be surprised the things we know and you don't.'

'You're all smart kids and the situation is simple.' Sherman unzipped his leather jacket, revealing twin holsters—one strapped under each arm. 'We need you to help us retrieve the data we came for. You need us to get you off this base before it blows up. End of story.'

'How do we know you won't kill us once you've got what you want?'

'Because we don't kill kids,' Darren said, glancing

sideways at Nulce. 'And because you're too valuable to the army.'

'So. Do we have a deal?' Sherman asked.

The boys looked at each other.

'We have a deal,' Jimmy replied.

PART 5

19.00 hours—20.00 hours

Reality is merely an illusion, although a very persistent one.

Albert Einstein

19.00

The boys had spent the last ten minutes getting a crash course in espionage. Nulce demonstrated how to load and fire his automatic weapon, though he insisted his team had no arms to spare.

'Where are *we* going to get guns from?' Barn asked.

'From the guys I kill,' Nulce answered simply.

Each of Sherman's team carried miniature computers called handcoms—and Darren showed the children how to operate them. The devices were more advanced than anything they'd ever seen but, in minutes, they had achieved an understanding of the handcom workings that a normal child would have taken weeks to learn.

'You guys really are smart,' Darren said approvingly.

In return, Dave and Simon tried to teach Sherman's team how the base schematics and personnel could be entered into a handcom and identified on its screen. They weren't nearly so fast at picking things up.

'We don't have time for this,' Sherman announced, after mistaking himself for a security camera twice in a row. 'You kids can operate the handcoms. We'll do the shooting.' He scratched his chin in exasperation and looked at Jimmy. 'Now what's the best way to proceed, in your expert opinion?'

'We should pair up,' Jimmy said without hesitation. 'One kid one adult. How you getting on with the Special Forces walkie-talkies, Simon?'

Simon looked up from the radio he was taking apart. Madrid had removed it from the body of Private Kruger.

'Each of Dunwoody's men has one of these. I've identified the frequency and I'll be able to use that to plot the whereabouts of every man. I'll feed their positions into the handcoms and they'll show up as black dots on the schematic of the base.' He stroked the handcom reverently. 'God, this is a fine piece of hardware.'

'What about you, Dave?'

'The base soldiers all have electronic identity tags, know? So we can track them too. I'll make them green dots.'

Darren looked even more impressed. Jimmy pointed to the little headsets that Sherman's team were wearing.

'And you've got these nifty communication devices, so I can use them to mark *our* positions. White dots, I think.' He smiled winningly at Nulce. 'After all, we're the good guys, aren't we?'

Nulce rolled his eyes.

'It's like a complicated game of chess, isn't it?' Jimmy continued. 'I say we play it that way—with our side directing where the other two sides should go.'

'And I suppose you'll be the one doing the

directing?' Sherman put his hands on his hips. 'You're probably a chess grandmaster or something.'

'Not me. I haven't got the patience.' Jimmy pointed to Barn, who was sitting on the floor drumming on his knees. 'But *he's* the best chess player I've ever seen.'

'There are 318,979,564,000 possible ways of playing the first four moves per side in a game of chess,' Barn said solemnly.

'Wait. Wait! You want the fat kid to come up with a strategy?' Nulce looked incredulously at Sherman. 'What kind of commander *are* you?'

Barn went bright red and stared at the ground. Sherman looked pained.

'You remind me of myself when I was young and stupid, Nulce,' he said sadly. 'Except I had looks and a personality.'

Darren coughed, hiding a smirk with his hand. Jimmy sat down next to Barn and gave him a handcom.

'Here's a cross section map of the base and the positions of the different groups. What would you think would be the best course of action?'

Barn looked at the mass of slowly moving dots on the screen. 'There are concentrations of base soldiers at the bottom of the stairwells on level three. But they can't get any further up because Dunwoody's men are at the top of those stairs. The black dots are totally outnumbered but only a handful of green dots can fit on the stairs at one time—so the black dots are able to hold the tops of each stairwell. And they've got a dozen men in

181

level one too—they'll be a back-up just in case May-Rose's forces do break through.'

'What about the three lifts?' Sherman asked.

'It would be suicide to use those,' Jimmy broke in. 'I'll bet Dunwoody's men have prised their doors open. If he was firing into the lift shaft, one gunman could keep a whole army at bay.'

Sherman chewed his lip thoughtfully. 'But Dunwoody's men can't get any further down, can they? There's enough of them to hold their positions but not enough to attack.'

'That's right,' Barn agreed. 'It's a stalemate.'

'What do you suggest?'

Barn wrinkled his brow. 'The black dots and the green dots both want to kill us. We can't get past them, and even if we could we'd never get back again.'

'I could have told you that,' Nulce grunted.

'Let's hear what the kid has to say,' Sherman said, shooting Nulce a warning glance. 'You can have my head examined when we get out.'

'We have to break the stalemate and get them all moving downwards, so that we can trap them in the lowest level, but I don't know how,' Barn protested, hugging his knees. 'I'm not smart like the rest of you.'

'Just treat it as a game.' Jimmy leaned close to Barn and put his arms around his beefy shoulders. 'Like it was your PlayStation or you were playing chess. Nobody has ever beaten you at either, have they? May-Rose doesn't even know *how* to play chess.'

'Aye? Well, I bet she does now,' Dave started, but Jimmy made a slicing motion with his hand to shut him up. Nulce gave a heartfelt groan.

Jimmy stood up and faced the baby-faced killer.

'And I wouldn't refer to Barn as the "fat kid" again,' he said with a wicked grin. 'Chess masters aren't afraid to sacrifice their own pieces to win. You might find yourself the first pawn removed from the game.'

Nulce held the boy's gaze, pure malice in his eyes.

'Enough. We'll play it by ear.' Sherman strode between Jimmy and Nulce. 'Mr Hicks, you're with me. Madrid, you take Simon. Darren, you're with the fa—I mean you go with Barn. Nulce and Dave will make up the last pair.'

'Dinnae try yir name callin' wi' me either, baby-face.' Dave wiggled his knife at Nulce. 'Or ye'll get malkied.'

'Say *what*?'

'Let's get moving before we end up killing each other,' Sherman snorted, holding out his hand to Dave. 'And give me that damned knife.' He grabbed the blade and stuck it in his pocket. 'The next kid, or adult, who gets lippy—I'll shoot them myself.'

'There's something odd about the green dots.' Barn was still studying the handcom. 'Why hasn't May-Rose told them to take off their security tags? I mean, she doesn't know you guys are here but, you know, just in case *Dunwoody's* men try to track them?'

'I hadn't thought of that,' Jimmy admitted.

'And how come there are so many of May-Rose's men still in the lowest level?' he continued.

'What do you think that means?' Darren asked gently.

'I'm not sure they *want* to get out.' The boy struggled to his feet and wrinkled his brow. 'It's like May-Rose is only *pretending* to try and escape—to keep Dunwoody's men defending the upper levels instead of attacking. Yes, that's it.' Barn's concentration was now absolute and he seemed hardly aware of the others in the room.

'She's *not* trying to get to the surface,' he said finally. 'She's keeping the Special Ops team from getting any further down because she's up to something else entirely.'

'Ah. So have ye got a plan now, big man?'

'Yes,' Barn said, surprised. 'I think I have.'

19.05

The party left the West Wing and trudged towards the main complex. The boys flinched every time they heard gunfire, but the adults ignored it. So did Barn, who was staring at the handcom as he walked, talking softly to himself.

There were only two buildings directly above the main complex, the Administration Block and the Maintenance and Vehicle Depot. The group stopped outside the main door of the latter.

'Now's the time for yir great strategy,' Dave said, nudging Barn. 'Nae pressure, like. It's just that all oor lives depend on it.'

Barn pulled at his lip. 'Mr Sherman, sir? You and Mr Nulce and Mr Darren should go with Dave and me into the Administration Block.'

'Darren is my *first* name,' said Darren.

'Yeah,' Madrid added. 'And if you call me missus you'll know all about it.'

'Yes, sir,' Barn replied uncertainly, and Madrid curled a pretty lip in resignation.

'What's in the Administration Block?' Sherman was peering round the corner of the Depot but there was no sign of life. Everyone was below ground, battling it out.

'Lift One,' Barn replied. 'It's the only lift that has a door above ground and it also stops at the

Ops Room on level one. We need to climb down the shaft and get out there.'

'I thought you said using the lifts was suicide?' Nulce protested. He was taking his rifle apart as he spoke, checking each part.

'It is for anyone trying to go *up*,' Barn insisted. 'But Dunwoody's men aren't expecting an attack force coming from above. According to the handcom they're only monitoring the shaft at level two. So we can climb out and into the Ops Room on level one without getting spotted. It has a reinforced door and nobody will even know we're in there.'

'We'll still be outnumbered.' Nulce was reassembling his gun with startling fluidity. 'Remember there's also a SWAT team in the corridors of level one and they've had time to build barricades. As soon as we leave the Ops Room they'll spot us and cut us down.'

'They won't be there,' Barn said confidently. 'A good chess player always creates a diversion before he can make a check.'

'What diversion is that?' Nulce scoffed. 'You gonna send Madrid down dressed as a schoolgirl?'

Madrid narrowed her eyes. 'Evolution just passed you by, Nulce, didn't it?'

Barn punched 1234 into the console beside the Vehicle and Maintenance Depot door and it slid silently open. The group found themselves looking at a long, concrete-floored garage. A dozen army trucks, draped in tarpaulin, lurked in the gloom. Barn pointed to a metal rectangle in the floor.

'That's a stairwell leading to level one. It has a blast-proof door but our code will open it. Madrid and Simon will go down that way.'

'Right into Dunwoody's men?' Simon said, taking a step back. 'What? You got something against me, Barn?'

'We'll send our pawns out in front of us,' Barn said simply. He pushed a switch on the wall and fluorescent strips in the roof sputtered into life. The entire garage was lit by a sickly white light.

'And those are your pawns,' the boy said, pointing to the far wall.

'Holy Hell,' Sherman breathed. 'What a stroke of brilliance.'

'Aw, man,' Dave choked out. 'That's awful cold!'

'Barn,' Jimmy said in a low voice. 'This is all wrong.'

'But that's what it will take to win the game,' the boy replied, hurt.

'You're not playing with chess pieces!' Simon looked appalled. 'We're talking about human lives!'

'These people will be dead in an hour anyway,' Sherman said. 'And none of you geniuses have got another plan.'

He stepped between Barn and his horrified companions.

'Well done, boy,' he said softly. 'We'll use the pawns.'

Lining the walls were dozens of metal drums filled with petrol.

19.10

Sherman led the others down the lift shaft. There was a small maintenance ladder set into the brickwork, which made the descent easier, but it was still tough going. Sherman and Nulce carried automatic weapons slung across their backs and the boys had the handcoms stuffed inside their jackets.

They were hampered further by the discovery that Dave had a paranoid fear of heights. Nulce had to keep hold of him as they descended and their progress through the claustrophobic darkness was punctuated by a stream of whispered Glaswegian curses.

'Will you shut up?' Nulce hissed. 'Why don't you send the enemy a goddamned postcard to say we're coming?'

'Keep yir shirt on, action man.' Dave was breathing like a steam train. 'I fall doon that shaft an' the whole base will ken aboot it.'

They finally reached the doors leading to the Ops Room. Darren and Barn took one side and Jimmy and Sherman the other. Sherman stuck his gun barrel into the small gap and together they levered the lift doors open and fell through.

'Oh, God,' Barn said, turning away.

Ops Room personnel were draped across consoles or sprawled on the floor like broken straws and the room was awash with gore. Dunwoody had been merciless in his execution of the occupants. Barn clapped a beefy hand over his mouth and tried not to gag.

'Ah'm gonnae sue the army over this.' Dave had swung out of the lift and into a pool of red. 'Ah've got blood all over mah Adidas, man.'

Nulce gave him a slap on the back and grinned approvingly at the boy.

19.13

Madrid and Simon were almost finished in the Maintenance Depot. They had punctured the fuel tanks of every vehicle and tipped over the oil drums. Now the concrete floor was a lake of petrol, shimmering under the fluorescent lights.

'You sure you want to do this?' Simon said, his voice muffled by an ill-fitting asbestos suit he had found in a locker. He was determined not to take any chances.

Madrid checked her handcom. 'Not really,' she said blankly. 'Then again, I don't want to die when this base blows up in forty-seven minutes.'

'Me neither.' The boy went to a panel on the wall and punched in 1234. 'I just don't know how I'll live with myself after this.'

The blast-proof doors in the floor were hidden by the reservoir of petrol, but it was easy to tell they were now open, for the level of black liquid began to rapidly go down.

Simon and Madrid waited until the petrol had almost leaked away. Then Madrid took out a lighter, flicked it to life and threw it onto the floor. A wave of blue flame raced across the concrete and they threw themselves behind a stack of truck tyres.

The blue flame vanished down the stairwell. There was silence for several seconds.

Then the shouting began.

19.15

On level one, Dunwoody's men were sheltering behind a barricade of filing cabinets, desks, and upended lab tables. It was a makeshift but adequate defence between themselves and any would-be attackers. But, as soon as the petrol began flowing down the stairs, the lieutenant knew his forces were doomed.

'Head for the Operations Room!' he shouted.

The men abandoned their positions and raced along the corridors, Dunwoody in the lead, waiting for that awful 'whump' that meant the petrol had been ignited. The passageway twisted and turned several times, studded with doors leading to labs and accommodation units, but he knew none of these would withstand the heat of an intense fire. The Ops Room, on the other hand, had reinforced doors in case of a terrorist attack— and Dunwoody had left them open. If his men could get there in time and force the doors shut they might survive.

The thought of sanctuary spurred him on and he sprinted round the last bend several feet ahead of the others.

He skidded to a halt.

'What the hell?'

The Operations Room doors were closed.

Dunwoody threw himself against them and his men joined in. They weren't just closed. They were sealed.

Behind them they heard the dull hiss of burning petrol.

'Down there!' Dunwoody pointed to the stairwell a few feet away.

His men took the stairs three at a time, some of them vaulting over the railings in their desperation to escape the advancing conflagration. His second force, barricaded on level two, looked up in astonishment as Dunwoody pelted down the steps and crashed into their makeshift fortifications.

'Down the next flight to level three,' he gasped. 'All of you!'

The soldiers looked at him in bewilderment. 'The base forces are at the bottom of the next stairwell,' one protested. 'There's dozens of them! We can barely hold our position as it is!'

'We've no choice!' Dunwoody cried, glancing back the way he had come. A torrent of burning petrol began pouring down the steps, oily smoke boiling above the flames.

'Sweet lord,' the soldier said. He turned to the others.

'What are you waiting for?' he roared. 'Let's take them!'

His men hoisted their weapons and leapt over the barricades. Dunwoody pulled out his pistol and joined their suicidal charge. Halfway down, a hail of bullets from below slammed into him and sent him catapulting over the rail.

He was dead before he hit the ground.

Screaming defiance, his condemned men thundered down the stairwell, firing as they went.

19.20

Sherman's team crouched behind desks in the Ops Room. They were joined by Madrid and Simon who had descended the lift shaft after completing their deadly task.

It wasn't a comforting place to shelter—though Nulce had made the best of it by reinforcing his makeshift barrier with corpses.

'Good job I grew up on a housing estate,' Dave whispered loudly. 'Or all this violence would have warped my fragile little mind.'

Nulce giggled.

'Will you shut up for once!' Simon shouted. 'I've just sent dozens of men to their deaths, for God's sake.'

'Away and boil yer heid, ya big jessie!' Dave snapped back. 'This is how I deal with it! Aw' right?'

Barn was sitting on the floor, tears streaming down his face.

'I did what you told me to do,' he sobbed. 'I just did what you told me to do.'

'What's happening with the fire?' Madrid hunkered down beside Jimmy.

'You're pretty emotionless, aren't you?' the boy said.

'I didn't join the army to win a popularity

194

contest,' she snapped curtly. 'Just tell me what's going on.'

Jimmy shone a torch on his handcom.

'The fire is now raging on level four and filtering into level five,' he said. 'The base soldiers have retreated to level six—the lowest level. There's only one staircase down to that area.'

'What about Dunwoody's force?'

'None of the black dots are moving. They were trapped between the fire and overwhelming numbers of base soldiers. They never stood a chance.' His hand trembled as he tried to hold the tiny computer steady. 'A lot of the green dots are stationary too. Dunwoody's guys must have put up quite a fight before they were killed.'

'How many base soldiers are still alive?'

'Fifty or sixty, I'd say. But not for much longer. That's why we're all hiding behind something.'

'Yeah? Why *is* that exactly?' Darren asked.

'Level five is burning. That's where experiments on alternative fuel cells take place. Highly combustible.' Jimmy slid down and put his arms over his head. 'The flames will be getting there just about now.'

'So keep down everyone,' Sherman began. 'We don't know how much com—' He didn't get to finish his sentence.

There was a massive boom from below them. Sherman's team and the boys gritted their teeth and covered their ears as a noise like a low-flying jet rocketed through the corridors. The solid steel doors of the Ops Room buckled like tin foil and a plume of yellow flame shot across the roof before being sucked back into the corridor.

'And then there were none,' Jimmy said sadly.

The rest lay in stunned silence. Finally Sherman raised his head.

'Status report,' he said, loudly to compensate for the ringing in his ears.

'None of the green dots are moving now,' Simon said in a cracked voice. 'They're all dead.'

'No they're not!' Jimmy was glaring at the handcom. 'The men in Bunker Ten are still alive.'

'How could *they* survive?'

'Bunker Ten contains the biohazard labs!' he replied. 'Any samples of infectious material or contaminants will be stored there, so they obviously have a blast-proof door. It's a cracker too, if it withstood that last explosion.'

'Damn! How will we get past it?'

'The sodjers inside winnae even die fae smoke inhalation,' Dave groaned. 'There are huge fans down there to stop any leaked viruses getting oot. They'll just sook the fumes away.'

'How many soldiers inside?'

'About twenty. And I bet May-Rose is with them.'

'Then its time we did *our* bit.' Sherman got unsteadily to his feet. 'Check your weapons.'

'The force of the explosion will have blown out the fire,' Jimmy said. 'We'll be able to start descending in a few minutes. Don't touch any metal surfaces, though, they'll still be too hot.'

'OK.' Sherman looked uneasily across at Barn.

The boy was making a strange gurgling sound, tears streaking down his blackened face. Blood was smeared across his forehead where a shard of flying metal from the door had grazed it.

'You all right, son?'

Barn shook his head slowly, his shoulders heaving. 'I killed all those people,' he moaned, rocking backwards and forwards. 'I'm going to hell.'

He looked around, eyes wide with terror, at the drifting smoke and dead bodies. 'I'm in hell *now*!'

He began to convulse violently, gulping in huge mouthfuls of air.

'Barn?'

'Man, he's havin' a fit!' Dave ran over and grabbed his friend by the shoulders. 'C'mon, big man! Keep the heid, eh? Ahm here. Dave's here!'

Barn's eyes began to roll back in his head.

'Aw no! Somebody dae something!'

Sherman took a shuddering breath and crawled over to them.

'Barn,' he said loudly, 'listen to me. You didn't kill anyone.' He pulled the shaking boy towards him and held him tightly against his chest. 'You didn't kill anyone, son. Not a soul.'

He gripped Barn as tightly as he could, rocking him back and forwards. Eventually the boy's shuddering abated and his breathing became normal.

'I didn't kill anyone?'

'You didn't,' Sherman repeated. 'This is just a simulation. None of it is real.'

19.22

'Sherman!' Darren's voice was strident. 'You can't tell them!'

'Tell us whit, man?'

'Yeah. Why not?' Nulce piped up. 'What the hell difference does it make?'

'Will you be all right?' Sherman asked Barn. 'I need to talk to the others.'

'I think so.' The boy looked at him tearfully. 'I trust you.'

Sherman swallowed hard.

'I'll be back in a minute.' He stood, wiped the boy's tears from his leather jacket and signalled to the others. 'The rest of you over here with me.'

They gathered round him. Barn sat on the floor a few feet away, lost in his own misery.

'This is a bad idea,' Darren griped in a low voice.

'Putting this guy in charge was a worse one,' Nulce mumbled.

'Erm . . . look . . . none of this is actually real,' Sherman said to the boys. He opened his arms to take in the room. 'All of this is a simulation.'

'Dinnae be daft, man.'

'He's right,' Darren said resignedly. 'This whole base is fake and . . . er . . . here's the hard part . . . so is everyone in it.'

The boys stared uncomprehendingly at him.

'I know you won't understand, but . . . oh, how do I tell you this?'

'You're not children,' Madrid said. 'You're characters in a simulation. Computer programs.'

'You trying to tell us we're not *real*?' Jimmy gaped incredulously.

'You're capable of independent thought,' Darren said. 'But essentially, yes, you're programmed to think and act as children. Very smart children. But you're actually pieces of very sophisticated circuitry.'

'Oh aye. An' I bet you leave oot eggs fur the Easter Bunny.'

'I do not *believe* I'm hearing this!' Simon's face was bright red behind the dirt. 'Are you completely insane? Of course this is real! I mean, right now I don't *want* it to be real . . . but it just *is*.'

'Ahm wi' Simon on this one.' Dave held up a bruised arm. 'This is way too sair tae be imaginary.'

'Calm down, you two.' Jimmy narrowed his eyes and jerked a thumb towards Barn. 'You want him to have another fit? Anyway, we're scientists, aren't we? Shouldn't be scared of weird ideas.'

'This isnae weird, man,' Dave hissed. 'It's pure mental.'

'Think about it.' Darren brushed ash from his shoulder. 'We suddenly appear from nowhere, in a top secret base, just at the right moment to save you.' He pointed to the handcom. 'We know all about your plan to escape and we've got technology more advanced than anything you've ever seen.'

The children pondered this with a sinking feeling.

'So why are you here?' Jimmy said. '*Supposing* you're telling the truth.'

'Because of May-Rose,' Darren said. 'She's a rogue program. Started off like you, but somehow she's become aware of what she really is.'

'So, she's reprogramming the other characters in this "game" in an attempt to do . . . what?'

'Get out and affect other computer systems, I imagine.' Darren looked around. 'We need a sample of her programming to find out for sure—what you would call her genetic make-up—and we need to get it before this whole place vanishes.'

'Before it blows up, ye mean?'

'Before the computer running the program shuts down.'

Dave gave a bark of laughter. 'You lot are absolutely oot-yer-face, nutters!'

'Feeling a bit insecure, shorty?' Nulce said snidely. 'Come on, geniuses. Why would we tell you this crap unless it was true?'

'What about your promise to help us escape?' Jimmy said bitterly.

'I'd save you if I knew how,' Sherman admitted guiltily. 'But I don't.'

'Sherman, they're just computer programs.' Nulce's voice dripped with scorn.

'Shut up, you,' Madrid snapped.

'Well, you don't have to believe me. I certainly wouldn't if I were you.' Sherman unfastened a small round object from his belt. 'Tell you what.

This is a grenade with a twist timer, simple to work. You've got half an hour. Get back to the surface, try to blast your way through the fences and good luck to you. We can handle things from here on out.'

'In case you'd forgotten, we're still outnumbered,' Madrid said coolly. 'And these kids now know how to fire a gun.'

'I have a son about your age.' Sherman ignored his subordinate and smiled at Jimmy. 'Looks a bit like you, in fact. We don't talk and I regret that.' He handed the disc to the boy. 'Go on. Get out of here.'

'Now ye've got *me* goin, eh?' Dave held up his hand. 'I cannae help thinking that aw' this time, May-Rose has stayed in Bunker Ten wi' her wee cronies instead of trying to work her way up the levels and escape. Whit does she know that we dinnae know, know?'

'Don't you start!' Simon threatened.

Jimmy thumped a fist into his palm. 'Maybe she's working on a different escape route.'

'Aye, but what's she gonnae do? Build a teleporter and transport herself tae the nearest tropical island?'

'Who knows?' Jimmy stood up. 'She's a super genius. Maybe that's exactly what she *is* doing.'

He crossed the Ops Room, threading his way past the broken bodies. On the far wall was a gun rack fitted with a row of automatic weapons. The personnel hadn't been able to reach them before Dunwoody cut them down.

'Look. Whether this *is* a game or reality, we'll never get out of range in half an hour. Our best shot at survival is to make it to Bunker Ten and find out what May-Rose is up to.'

He pulled a rifle from the rack and looked along the barrel, more for effect than anything else. He'd never pulled a trigger in his life.

'Hey, Barn,' he shouted. The boy looked up, eyes widening in his streaky face, and raised his arms in surrender.

'Put your hands down.' Jimmy tutted. 'Sherman's right. We're in a virtual simulation. You haven't killed anyone.'

'Really?'

'Trust me. It's just a game.' Jimmy gave the boy a jovial wink.

'Hicks!' Simon hissed. 'What are you playing at?'

'You want him to have another fit?' Jimmy muttered out of the side of his mouth. He stuffed the bomb in his pack and tossed the rucksack to Barn. 'You carry this, OK? I'll take the gun.'

Barn nodded, managing a sorrowful smile. Jimmy slung the rifle round his own neck.

'Let's go finish what we started.'

19.25

Sherman split his force into the same four pairs. The corridors were hot and suffocatingly smoky, but the fire had been extinguished by the explosion, just as Jimmy predicted.

Sherman and Jimmy Hicks climbed into the lift shaft once more. This time there was no chance of them being spotted as they went down. Even if they could be seen through the smoke, nobody was guarding the elevators any more. They kept in touch with the others by using the miniature head-pieces and handcoms.

The shaft was filled with acrid smoke and a dull glow emanated from the bottom where a pocket of flaming petrol still burned.

It looked like the passageway to Hell.

The rest of the team made their way along the corridors of level one, shining flashlights in front of them. The boys carried the handcoms and the adults carried the firearms. Madrid and Simon took stairwell one and Darren and Barn stairway two. Nulce and Dave continued to the other end of the corridor and began to climb down the second lift shaft.

Barn was once again in charge of operations, peering through the gloom at his handcom and guiding the others using Darren's headset. A few of the green dots on level four and five had begun to move again. Some base soldiers had obviously survived the blast—perhaps they had been sheltering behind heavy equipment when the explosion occurred.

Barn moved Sherman's team around like the chess master he was, directing them along the smoke-shrouded passageways and in and out of shattered rooms. They easily outmanoeuvred the base soldiers, trapping them between pairs and dispatching them with quick, efficient bursts of gunfire. Within a few minutes they had made their way to level five and Barn and Darren were descending the stairway to level six—the lowest level.

'Shouldn't we wait for the others?' Darren peered into the dark stairwell and cocked his gun. 'I'm not much of a fighter.'

Barn checked the computer in his hand yet again.

'The enemy are all in Bunker Ten right at the other end of the level,' he said. 'But it's safer if you wait downstairs because there's a couple of base soldiers still loose on level five. I'll send Madrid and Nulce towards them but I'll have to do it from up here—the reception on these headsets is fading the lower we get.'

'You be careful then,' Darren warned. He gave Barn a friendly pat on the cheek and made his way cautiously down the stairs.

Like the rest of the underground complex, the lights on level six had been destroyed by the blast—though Jimmy insisted that power would be unaffected in the biohazard labs. An operation of that sort would have its own generators to keep the reinforced doors sealed and the lights and fans working.

Darren wouldn't have minded getting near those fans. The smoke was gradually fading—being replaced by another acrid smell whose origins he tried not to think about.

He turned and shone the flashlight beam in the direction of Bunker 10.

Four men stood facing him, rifles in their hands.

Darren drew a sharp breath, his heart hammering.

'Barn?' he said quietly into the intercom. There was no answer.

'Put down your weapon and come with us.' One of the base soldiers motioned towards the biohazard area with his gun.

'*She's* waiting for you.'

19.27

The others found Barn sitting at the top of the stairs that led down to the lowest level.

'Hey, big man.' Dave slapped the boy on the leg. 'Where's yer skinny pal?'

Barn didn't speak. He was shining the torch on his watch.

'Where's Darren, Barn?' Sherman repeated, an edge to his voice.

'May-Rose's men captured him,' the boy replied, turning to the handcom. 'They're taking him to Bunker Ten.'

'What! How could you let that happen?' Jimmy stepped forward, looking around.

'Where's my pack, Barn? Where's my pack with the explosive device in it?'

'Darren's carrying it.' The boy tapped his watch. 'See . . . the doors protecting the biohazard units are obviously bomb proof from the outside. We have to blow them from the inside.'

There was a resounding detonation from under them and the floor shuddered. A water pipe burst in the darkness behind them, hissing into the corridor.

'The door will be open now,' Barn said.

Sherman's mouth dropped open. 'You sacrificed *Darren*?'

Barn looked puzzled. 'It's just a *game*.'

Jimmy fixed Sherman with a steely gaze. 'Can't have it both ways, Mr Sherman.'

'You kids are something else,' Nulce said nonchalantly. Sherman was shaking all over.

'My God, you really are monsters,' he spat.

'Ye telt Barn he wasnae daen nothin' wrang, ya big tube,' Dave snarled back. 'Now yir mad 'cause he believed you?'

'Hey! Recriminations can come later,' Madrid said. 'The boy's evened the odds.'

Before there could be any more arguments she unshouldered her gun and began moving down the stairs.

19.30

Madrid and Nulce led the final charge. There was no point in hiding any more, no element of surprise on their side. It was a straight-out fight.

Each member of the team had switched their headsets to loud static, in case they encountered May-Rose. This was no handicap to trained combatants like Madrid and Nulce, who relied on hand signals when in action. They reached the reinforced doors leading to Bunker 10 and found them torn apart by the bomb Darren had unwittingly carried to his death. Both dived through the gap.

Madrid was like an iron butterfly, drifting elegantly from doorway to doorway, unleashing long bursts of automatic fire down the corridor. Nulce weaved and bobbed like a deadly bee, pitching into rooms and crisscrossing through them, raking the area with bullets. Sherman stayed close behind, covering their backs and sheltering the boys in case Nulce and Madrid had missed anyone lurking in the dark.

The remaining base forces didn't stand a chance. Unable to resist May-Rose's orders, they refused to retreat—but they were disoriented by the fire, the explosions, and the smoke and in no state to mount a proper defence.

Within minutes the last of the soldiers were dead and the group halted outside the final door. On the wall was a stark warning.

CAUTION BIOHAZARD

BIOSAFETY CHAMBERS

AIR LOCK DOOR/DECON SHOWER

DO NOT ENTER WITHOUT WEARING A BIOHAZARD SUIT

The adults looked at each other nervously. Jimmy signalled for them to turn off the static on their headsets.

'Any infectious material will be in sealed containers in a titanium containment room,' he said quietly. 'Don't worry, May-Rose can't let any kind of toxin loose without killing herself.'

'Get ready to cover me.' Madrid switched the static back on and punched 1234 into the console set in the wall. The door slid open and she vaulted through. With a roar of bravado, Nulce leapt after her, rolling as he hit the floor on the other side. They ran the length of the decontamination corridor and vanished through a curtain made of plastic strips.

'Bloody cowboys,' Sherman complained, signalling for the boys to follow him.

Bunker 10 had survived the blast entirely. Fluorescent tubes in the ceiling lit up the room and fans whirred in the walls.

May-Rose was standing in the middle of the lab, her hands above her head in surrender. Madrid covered her from a safe distance, static turned up to full blast, while Nulce got behind the girl and forced her to her knees. With practised moves he fastened her hands behind her back using lab gauze, tied a strip across her mouth and stepped back to admire his work.

The rest of the party removed their headsets.

'There now, wasn't that easy?' Nulce said sarcastically.

The children stared at their former friend. She looked tiny and lost and it was impossible to reconcile the forlorn figure in the yellow dress with the carnage they had witnessed.

'Guys. Look over there.' Simon pointed with a trembling finger.

Behind May-Rose was a huge contraption resembling a giant turbine engine. It was covered in wires and humming with energy.

It was a monster-sized version of the Machine in their dormitory.

'Holy Hell,' Jimmy said. 'She's built a time machine.'

'A what?' Sherman shook his head in disbelief. 'Don't be stupid!'

'Why not?' Simon insisted. 'We were working on the time travel theories together in our spare time.'

'But it was you who made the breakthrough,' Jimmy said. 'Not May-Rose.'

Simon turned red.

'I was using *her* notes,' he whispered. 'She left them lying on her desk when she went to work in Bunker Ten.'

'You sneaky wee bissom.' Dave punched his companion on the arm.

'I would never have had the smarts to make a machine that would actually work.' He pointed to the captive girl. 'But now May-Rose has an intellect that dwarfs ours. She hasn't just worked out the same formula as me—she's actually put it into practice.'

'That's how she intended to escape,' Jimmy said. 'She was going to send herself through time.'

'Eh?' Nulce spluttered. 'I say we shoot these kids right this minute.'

'Look!' Sherman cut through the argument. 'I'm sorry, guys, but this is ridiculous!'

'You got a better explanation?' Simon sneered. 'What the hell do *you* think this contraption does?'

'You are computer simulations! You *have* to accept that!' Sherman clapped his hands to his face and sighed. 'This is . . . it . . . must be a device to transfer May-Rose's program to other computer systems.' He walked around the Machine glowering at it. 'God, I *hate* technology.'

'Oh. And *that* doesn't sound far-fetched!' Jimmy retorted.

Dave strolled over to Nulce who was guarding May-Rose. 'You were right, Nulcy Boy,' he frowned. 'This *was* too easy.'

'*Nulcy Boy*? Do you *want* to get shot?' But Dave had turned away, tapping his lip in consternation.

'Jimmy,' he said suddenly, 'did you not say that infectious materials are kept in a titanium containment room?'

'That's right.'

'Wouldn't titanium block any life signs showing up on the handcoms?'

'Yes it would. Now drop your weapons and put your hands behind your heads.'

The others spun round at the sound of the voice. Nulce swore loudly and threw down his gun like a petulant child.

The door to the containment room was now open and Doctor Monk was standing at the entrance, pointing a rifle at Madrid's head.

19.35

Monk strode over to May-Rose, rifle still trained on Madrid, and yanked loose the girl's gag. He moved in a precise, determined way as if something else were directing his actions.

'Thank you, doctor,' the girl said. She struggled to her feet and drew herself up to her full height of four feet one.

Then the voice came billowing out of her frail, child's body.

'The rest of you will not harm me or Doctor Monk. You will not run from me. You will do whatever I say.' She gave a small smile. 'Get into a straight line. Eyes front.'

The boys gasped in dismay as each of them shuffled into line like soldiers on parade. They had no control whatsoever over their actions. May-Rose giggled.

'Just testing.'

Doctor Monk untied the child's wrists. Absently rubbing them she strolled along the line as if she were a miniature general inspecting her troops.

'I've been waiting for you, Jimmy,' she said agreeably. 'I had faith that you'd get here. All right, you've cut it a bit fine, but you made it.'

'What the hell is she talking about?' Nulce tried to turn his head but it refused to move.

'You think I couldn't have outsmarted Dunwoody's men and reached the surface?' May-Rose scoffed. 'Then what? I'd have lost most of my force getting past him and the rest would have fallen at the perimeter fences. If I got through, I'd have to traverse miles of forest in minus temperatures and thick snow, with the army and the air force hunting me all the way. I probably wouldn't make it past the blast perimeter before this place went up. What I have inside me is too important to risk like that.'

'What do you have inside you, May-Rose?' Jimmy asked.

'The future,' she replied.

'I don't understand.'

'Yes you do,' the girl smirked. 'I'm carrying an entirely new genetic strain.' She moved down the line again looking closely at Dave and Simon.

'All living things are controlled by their genes. They hunt, kill, and compete so that the strongest genes will survive. That's as it should be. The way it's always been.'

She pursed her lips in a childish pout.

'But humanity keeps trying to rise *above* its genetic programming. You allow the weak to survive. You form societies where those with inferior genes are able to live.'

'So yer no' a fan o' wheelchair ramps,' Dave said defiantly. 'Get tae the point.'

'You even try to manipulate your own genetic material. Bend it to your will.' A note of outrage had crept into the child's voice. 'Genes are not your playthings! Genes are your masters!'

'We didn't know what we were dealing with.' Monk spoke in a faraway, monotone voice. 'We created our own Frankenstein's monster.'

'What are they talking about?' Nulce hissed to Madrid. But the blonde was listening intently to May-Rose and the doctor.

'May-Rose is the host for a new strain of gene,' the doctor said blankly. 'One that's a lot stronger than before.'

'So strong that you're no longer in charge of your own lives,' Jimmy spat.

'Enough. I intend to transform all of you too.' May-Rose smiled broadly, revealing perfect white teeth. 'We'll use the Machine to travel to a point in the future where Pinegrove doesn't exist. Where nobody will believe a group of children can cause them any harm. You're already geniuses. With my genes inside, you'll become an unstoppable force.'

'And we spread the disease?'

'You call it a disease. I call it a cure.' May-Rose moved along the line to Jimmy, stood on tiptoe and peered into the boy's eyes. 'Did you really think humanity could force nature to its knees?'

'I was hoping that, eventually, we would.'

'Your arrogance is breathtaking as usual, Jimmy.' May-Rose moved further along the line to Sherman and Madrid. 'Once I have injected you with my genetic material, then you, Simon, David, Barn, and Lesley will change the world—just like you always wanted.'

Jimmy shook his head angrily. 'Not Lesley. Lesley escaped.'

'Don't be silly.' May-Rose stopped in front of Madrid. The woman was still rigid, staring over the little girl's head.

'*This* is Lesley.'

19.37

Jimmy tried to turn his head and look at Madrid, but his body refused to obey. The boy's stomach was churning.

'She must have come back through time to save you, Jimmy,' May-Rose said. 'Can't think of any other explanation. She came back through time, even though she knew the past can't be changed. That's the kind of stupidity I *will* see wiped out.'

'Just wait a goddamned minute!' Nulce was struggling against the invisible bond that held him. 'We *didn't* come back through time! The year is 2027 and this is a damned computer simulation!'

'Is that what you were told?' May-Rose sneered. 'You were double-crossed, you moron. This is 2007, twenty years earlier than you think, and everything around you is very real.'

'You are a self-delusional, insane little girl,' Nulce yelled. 'No! You're not even that! You're a computer program, who can't accept the fact!' He tried to fling himself forward and even moved a few inches. Monk swung his gun to cover the raging man.

Sherman launched himself at the doctor. He collided with Monk and both men sprawled across the floor, wrestling for the gun.

217

'Stop it! STOP IT RIGHT NOW!' May-Rose roared at Sherman—but her terrible voice seemed to have no effect on him.

The others watched helplessly, unable to come to Sherman's aid, as the men rolled backwards and forwards clawing at each other. Sherman threw his head forwards and butted Monk in the face. The doctor slammed a fist into Sherman's throat and he jerked backwards, gasping for breath. In that split second Monk swept the gun up from the floor and pulled the trigger, but Sherman twisted out of the line of fire and thumped the barrel away with the palm of his hand. Monk hit Sherman across the throat again.

'Stop *doing* that!' Sherman rasped, pulling Dave's knife from inside his jacket. He slammed an elbow into Monk's face and, as the doctor recoiled, thrust the blade deep into his adversary's chest.

With a slow, gurgling sound, Doctor Monk sank back and died.

Sherman jerked round, still holding the knife.

May-Rose was standing over him clutching at the bullet hole in her throat, a red flower of blood seeping down onto her yellow dress. Silently she sank to her knees, her mouth trembling. The others suddenly found themselves able to move again.

'Aw, Jesus, I'm sorry, kid!' Sherman grabbed the girl round the waist and tried to pull her upright. Her head lolled to one side, eyes vacant. 'I was just trying to get the gun. I didn't mean . . .'

'She's dead, Sherman.' Madrid came over, lifted

May-Rose from her leader's arms and laid her gently on the floor.

'How the hell were you able to fight?' Nulce demanded, unaffected by the girl's death. 'I couldn't even move a muscle.'

'I wear a miniature hearing aid,' Sherman said wearily. 'You squeeze to switch it on and off.' He put his hands behind his head in mock surrender and tapped the lobe of his ear. 'I can lip read but, without it, I'm deaf as a post.'

Nulce snorted. 'I *knew* there was a reason Colonel Cruikshank picked a loser like you to lead the team.'

'Did you say Colonel *Cruikshank*?' Jimmy gasped. But Nulce was looking at his watch.

'Hell! We only got twenty minutes to complete our mission,' he announced. He picked up a gun and strode towards the containment room. 'The MR12 sample must be in here.'

'You have some explaining to do, Madrid,' Sherman said bitterly.

The woman sat down on a bench and put her head in her hands. Jimmy walked over and stood in front of her.

'You're *Lesley*?'

Madrid nodded, not looking up. Simon, Dave, and Barn crowded round her.

'You look different, doll. Mair mature, know?'

'I stopped dying my hair,' she muttered.

'Hey! Who the hell is Lesley?' Sherman was trying to wipe May-Rose's blood from his hands. 'Will you tell these kids who you are? Madrid?'

'Sherman, in 2007 I escaped from Pinegrove Military Installation right before it blew up. So did a boy called Cruikshank. We were both fourteen—protégés like these kids here. The army picked us up, but I didn't know what had happened and Cruikshank claimed he didn't either. So the army kept us on. Cruikshank grew up and eventually became a colonel. Pinegrove was rebuilt, and he was put in charge of it.'

'They rebuilt Pinegrove?' Simon moaned. 'Wasn't it unlucky enough the first time?'

'What happened to you?' Jimmy asked.

'I was billeted in England and I never saw Cruikshank again.' Madrid finally looked up, transferring her gaze from floor to ceiling. 'I worked as an army researcher for years. Didn't really know anything else. I met a lieutenant, fell in love, got married and had a little girl.' Madrid had begun to blink rapidly.

Jimmy gave a wounded gasp. There were clinking sounds from inside the containment unit as Nulce moved samples around, looking for the one he had been sent to find. Sherman had forgotten about the blood and was listening in bewilderment.

'My husband and child were killed in a car crash.' Madrid's voice was hypnotic. 'After that I started volunteering for . . . special missions.'

The others looked shocked but there was no emotion in Madrid's voice. 'I worked my way up pretty high in counter-terrorism. I actually hold a higher rank than Cruikshank.'

'Is *this* a special mission?'

'I got to hear about Cruikshank's new "simulation" and it suddenly clicked with me what he was *really* up to. When he left Pinegrove as a child and stole the time travel formula, he must have hid it before the army picked him up and then retrieved it again. It took him twenty years to build a Machine that worked.' She laughed miserably and glanced at the larger version humming in the corner. 'May-Rose managed to build one in six hours.'

'All this to get a sample of May-Rose's genetic material and leave it in a *well*?' Sherman looked incredulous. 'Why?'

'Because he could dig it up twenty years later,' Dave volunteered. 'It's gonnae be worth a lot o' dosh.'

'The guy had invented a working time machine!' Simon countered. 'What could be worth more than that?'

'I don't *know* his reasons,' Madrid admitted. 'Never got time to find out. All I managed to do was pull a few strings and get on his team. He didn't recognize me.' She looked down at herself. 'I had a code name and I'd changed a lot since I was a girl.'

'So this *isn't* a virtual simulation?' Sherman was still trying to come to terms with these revelations. 'You're telling me we've really been sent back in time?'

'That's what I'm telling you.'

'How are we supposed to get back?'

'We can't, Sherman.' The woman turned her steely gaze towards him. 'The Machine can send things forward in time or it can send them back—but it's a one way trip, whichever direction you go. That's why Cruikshank wanted you to put the DNA sample in the well, so he could retrieve it in the future. There's no way we could bring it back ourselves.'

'What if we try and get off the base now?'

'We won't make it. Pinegrove blows up in 2007 and there *are* no survivors. If we got out then everything we did from that point on would change the future. Cruikshank wouldn't invent a time machine. We wouldn't *be* here. But we are. It's called a time travel paradox.'

'Cruikshank *knew* we'd never get out?'

'Yes.'

'And so did *you*?'

Madrid nodded again. 'You don't join the army unless you're prepared to sacrifice yourself.'

'I'm not *in* the army,' Sherman said bitterly. 'I test computer games.'

'Then pass this test, for God's sake!' Nulce was in the doorway, a stoppered glass vial in his hand. On the side was a label, with MR12 handwritten on the side. 'I can't believe you're falling for these lies! Let's complete our mission, and get the hell out of here.'

'You heard Madrid. We're trapped.'

'No wait!' Jimmy interrupted. 'We can use May-Rose's machine to send *ourselves* into the future! As long as we go more than twenty years forward in time, *after* Cruikshank invents his machine, there'll be no paradox. Everyone will think we died in the explosion, because there'll be no record of us—but we'll have got away!'

'Will you get a grip? There is no such thing as time travel!' Nulce waved his gun at the Machine. 'That's some contraption May-Rose was building to infect other computers with her virus!'

He held out a despairing hand to Sherman. 'Colonel Cruikshank told us not to believe anything the kids said. He *told* us they'd do this.'

He swung the gun menacingly towards the boys. They shuffled nervously behind Madrid—all except Jimmy, who moved protectively in front of her. Madrid hesitated then gently put a hand on his shoulder.

'Madrid is one of us,' Sherman said slowly. 'Put that gun up, mister.'

'We don't know *who* she is!' Nulce's voice now had an edge of panic to it. 'What about the colonel's investors? For all we know she's working for the competition. She could be a double agent.'

'Nulce, these kids are offering us a way out, despite all we've done.'

'She's trying to make us fail.' The gun was trembling in Nulce's hand, but his eyes glittered with an icy calm. 'I *never* fail.'

And he pulled the trigger.

Sherman hurled himself sideways. The burst caught him square in the chest and threw him halfway across the room. Madrid swung Jimmy away and scooped up her own gun in one fluid movement. She returned fire, but Nulce had vanished into the decontamination corridor. They heard the echoes of his running footsteps fading away as he headed back towards the surface.

The others ran and knelt beside Sherman. He lay on his side, a midnight patch spreading across his black jumper and oozing over the arm of his leather jacket. He coughed and a trickle of red bubbled out of his mouth.

'Sherman, you idiot,' Madrid said, gently wiping away the blood. 'I *told* you this wasn't a game.'

Sherman reached out and took Jimmy's hand.

'If you get out would you find my kid?' A tear rolled down his cheek and he grimaced in pain. 'Would you tell him how I died?' He coughed once more and closed his eyes.

'I'll find him and I'll tell him. I promise.' Jimmy squeezed the man's callused hand. 'Please don't die.'

'I'm so tired of games,' Sherman whispered lying back. He breathed out once, as light as a bird's wing fluttering.

Then he was dead.

19.40

Madrid kissed the lifeless man softly on the cheek. Jimmy and Dave looked away. Barn was crying quietly. Holding back his own tears, Simon walked over to the Machine and began tapping at the dials.

Madrid looked up, shifting to her cold, calm persona with frightening ease. 'Think you can make that do what it's supposed to?'

'It's just a glorified version of the Machine in our dormitory—except this one works.' Simon picked up a pad and looked at a screed of formulae May-Rose had scribbled across it. 'I can calculate how to set it, yeah.'

'You need to send us at least twenty years into the future,' Jimmy said. 'According to history, we don't show up anywhere in the next two decades, so if we try to turn up any earlier it's a fair bet we don't make it. We'd land in the middle of the Atlantic Ocean or something.'

'That's the problem,' Simon said. 'I can send us to whatever time I like, but where am I sending us? I mean, the whole planet is turning and travelling through space.'

'Talking of time, lads.' Dave tapped his big gold watch. 'We've only got fifteen minutes left.'

'May-Rose had an intellect that defied belief,'

Jimmy said. 'She would have factored spatial adjustments into her calculations. I imagine we'll end up somewhere remote. Somewhere unlikely to have a shopping centre built over it years from now.'

'God, she did a good job on this.' Simon entered some final numbers into a keyboard on the side of the Machine. 'There. As far as I can tell, it's now set to transport us to an unknown location in 2028—twenty-one years from now.'

'Let's hope it's Barbados, man. I'm sorely needin' a week aff.'

Simon flipped a switch and, like an eye opening, a shimmering blue oval appeared in the centre of the room.

'I don't know how long this thing will stay open,' he urged. 'Which lunatic's going to be first?'

The boys stared apprehensively at the pulsating fissure. Dave stuck out his pigeon chest.

'Jimmy, Simon. See yous on the ither side. I'll get the tea on. C'mon, Barn.' He grabbed the large boy abruptly by the collar and pulled him through the hole. It rippled like an upright pond and grew calm again.

'Holy hell.'

Madrid tapped Jimmy on the arm. 'You ready, kid?'

'Don't call me kid.' Jimmy Hicks squared his shoulders. 'Look. Just in case we don't make it, I have to know. Why did you come back? You weren't aware of this Machine and you were sure you couldn't save us. So why?'

Madrid chewed her lip, thinking. Finally she spoke, though she still wouldn't look at the boy.

'I lost my husband and my only child.' She gave a wistful smile. 'I wasn't going to lose my first love without putting up a hell of a fight.'

She leaned forwards, as if to kiss him and then recoiled, shaking her head. The mask of indifference that covered her vulnerability slipped back on.

'You know what?' Simon said suddenly. 'I have a weird idea. What if I send Lesley *forty-one* years into the future instead of twenty-one, like the rest of you?' He pointed to Jimmy. 'You go twenty-one years into the future, age normally and, twenty years later, when Lesley appears, you'll be the same age.'

'You can *do* that?'

'Sure. May-Rose made this thing simpler to set than an alarm clock.'

Jimmy clasped his hands together and turned to Madrid.

'What? Would you? I mean . . . ' He shook his head, lost for words.

'Makes no difference to me where I go, or when.' Madrid shrugged. 'I'd say my career in the army was pretty much over. And my life was hardly a barrel of laughs.'

'Then I'll be at the Ranger Station just outside Pinegrove. Christmas Day, two o'clock, 2048.'

'Yeah? You stood me up last time.'

'Boy, you hold a grudge for a long time.'

'Jimmy, this is ridiculous.'

'It's a date.' The boy held up his hand to deter further argument. 'See you on the other side, Simon.'

He winked at Madrid.

'Two o'clock, 2048. I know how bad your memory is, but I'll be there.' Before the woman could object, he stepped into the portal and vanished.

'Oh, my God,' Madrid said, clasping a hand to her forehead. 'I don't believe that just happened.'

'Hey. Earth to Madrid.' Simon was already back fiddling with the Machine. 'I got a question. How did Cruikshank manage to send you back in time so accurately? He's smart but he's not in the same league as May-Rose.'

'He had something to aim at.' Madrid sat down and began looking at the girl's notes. 'The little transmitter that Jimmy gave him was in the pocket of his lab coat, the one he dropped just outside the fence when he ran from Pinegrove. He knew it was there and he homed in on that. That's why we couldn't arrive any earlier.'

'I should have guessed what May-Rose was up to.' Simon bent close and made a few more adjustments. 'Her notes about the Machine were much better than mine.' The boy straightened up. 'If someone like me could work out the formula for stripped light, then it would have been child's play for her to do the same and build a working model.'

'Don't put yourself down.' Madrid waved the notes at Simon. 'You came up with the formula independently and I'll vouch for that. After all, I was there.'

'Finished.' Simon wiped sweaty hands on his jeans. 'You go through, and I'll calibrate the machine back to the way it was, step into the hole and join the others.'

Madrid took a last look round. May-Rose lay between Sherman and Monk, dwarfed by the men, her hands folded over her chest.

'Hold on a second.'

'What is it?'

'This place is going to blow up in a few minutes and the blast destroys *acres* of land. If the Machine is still on, the explosion will follow you through the hole. None of you will get far enough away to survive the blast.'

'I know.' The boy came over and took the notes from Madrid. 'I imagine that May-Rose had conditioned Doctor Monk to stay behind and switch off the Machine.'

'But there's nobody alive to do it now.'

'Yes there is,' Simon said. 'Me.'

And he shoved Madrid with all his strength.

With a surprised yelp, she staggered backwards and vanished through the portal. May-Rose's time travel notes wafted through the air like paper doves and drifted gently to the floor.

Simon gave them a sorrowful kick.

'There goes my Nobel Prize,' he said in a small voice. 'But nobody should have ever discovered this.'

Then he switched off the Machine.

* * *

Simon made his way to the upper levels. Level one contained a dozen virtual simulation rooms, high enough up to have escaped the worst effects of the fire. The boy entered one and punched 1234 into the wall console.

'Run virtual simulation 24.12.07. *Christmas Party for the Pinegrove Gang,*' he said.

The room was suddenly transformed. It was now the kids' dormitory—but not the way it had looked that morning. In the centre of the room stood a beautiful Christmas tree, at least six feet high, decorated with old-fashioned wooden ornaments, wrapped in thick tinsel strands, and dotted with real candles in silver holders. There were brightly wrapped presents strewn around and paper lanterns hanging from the roof.

'Populate with simulated characters,' Simon commanded.

Jimmy and Lesley appeared, then Dave and Barn. Even Cruikshank and May-Rose were there. All were laughing and joking, opening presents and pulling crackers. Jimmy waved to him, one arm round Lesley's shoulder.

'Merry Christmas, Simon!' he grinned.

'You too, guys.' Simon sat down beside them and put on a paper hat. 'You too, wherever you are.'

19.57

Nulce plunged through the trees, kicking up gouts of snow as he ran. A pall of smoke rose behind him, polluting the night sky, and he could smell it drifting over the forest like a sooty rag. He broke into a clearing, consulted his handcom and gave a grunt of satisfaction.

In the middle of this glade was the well, covered by a sheet of corrugated iron.

Sobbing with relief, Nulce trudged to the centre of the gap and found the black box they had left earlier. He brought out the sample of MR12, inserted it carefully into one of his gloves and placed the glove in the lead box. He punched in a random security code to seal the box and slid the metal cover from the well. Taking a piece of rope, he lay down next to the lip, lowered the box to the bottom, and let go.

Out of the corner of his eye, he caught a minuscule movement. He slowly turned his head.

A white mouse was watching him from a few metres away, almost invisible against the snow. Nulce wouldn't have spotted it if it hadn't been for the red eyes. The tiny creature was quivering from head to foot and was obviously dying from cold. It looked like a lab mouse but Nulce couldn't see how that was possible. No cage-bred lab mouse would have braved these conditions or got this far.

The creature skittered over to the lip of the well. Then, just as suddenly, it plunged into the darkness.

Nulce gave a little start. He stood up and patted snow from his uniform, then looked up at the sky. The smoke had blocked out all the stars. With a last glance into the abyss, he slid the cover back over the well and pressed the recall button on the handcom.

'All right, Colonel,' he said. 'I completed the mission. Now get me out of here.'

There was silence. The only sound was his own breathing.

'Colonel? Colonel Cruikshank?' He shook the handcom. 'I completed the game! I completed it with forty seconds to spare!'

There was no answer.

A wind blew through the trees. Nulce stood up and began to curse. Then he pleaded. Finally he raised his hands above his head and screamed his rage.

He was still railing into the black night when an enormous ball of fire tore Pinegrove apart and whisked him out of existence.

PINEGROVE MILITARY INSTALLATION

Tuesday, 24 December 2027

The past does not repeat itself, but it rhymes.

Mark Twain

20.00

Heavy equipment had been excavating the ground all morning and soldiers with scoops, spades, and drills swarmed over the area like termites, hacking at the soil and carrying it away. The atmosphere was tense. The old well had been hidden for twenty years—buried by an explosion that had destroyed the original Pinegrove base. Now, for no reason that any of his men could fathom, Colonel Cruikshank was trying to uncover it and had put everyone on high alert.

They obeyed him without question, however. Everybody knew that the colonel was no fool.

Whenever the soldiers encountered large rocks, they used blasting caps to shear them apart, and frequent explosions scattered rooks from the surrounding trees. Once darkness fell, poles had been erected all round the area and massive floodlights attached so the excavations could continue.

Cruikshank was in the command tent when his handcom bleeped.

'Yes?'

It was his second-in-command. 'Sappers have found the well, sir. They've removed the cover and I've sent one down to make sure there's no blockage in the shaft.'

'I'll be right there.' Cruikshank put on a helmet

with a Davy lamp on the front and left the tent. The well was surrounded by curious soldiers but the colonel waved them away. He lowered himself over the lip of the hole and grasped the rope ladder fastened to the side.

'Don't touch anything!' he shouted to the bobbing light below. 'I'm coming down.'

A lone sapper was crouching at the bottom of the well. He too was wearing a helmet light and sifting through the dirt with a hand trowel and sieve. A pick, shovel, and a bag of blasting caps were lying next to the wall.

'Brought my gear just in case, but the shaft's completely clear.' The sapper gave a preoccupied salute and played his light around. A tangle of withered brown stalks tipped with thorns latticed the walls of the ancient stonework. 'Apart from those bloody bushes, though. They're all over the shop. I've cleared the worst of them away but they cut me to ribbons doing it.'

'You find anything unusual?' Cruikshank said curtly. He was quivering all over in anticipation.

'A small lead box, with a combination lock on the front. But it's open.'

'Open?' Cruikshank felt his heart lurch.

'Yeah. Hasn't been forced or anything.' The sapper shifted his light to a dark square shape lying in the dirt. 'No sign of damage, so it must have been opened using the combination.'

'Was there anything inside it?' The inside of Cruikshank's mouth was so dry he could hardly talk.

'A reinforced glass vial. Looks like it had a seal or a stopper in it at one time, but it's been . . . er . . . '

'Been what, soldier?' Cruikshank snapped.

'Looks like it's been chewed through,' the sapper said. 'Must have been this feller, I guess.' He shone the beam a few inches to the left.

Cruikshank almost fainted.

Poking out through the earth was the skeleton of a mouse.

'Don't see how a mouse could have got into a combination safe though, not unless he punched in the numbers with his wee paws.' The sapper gave a soft laugh. 'That'd have to be an awful smart mousy, eh? But whatever was in the vial has leaked away into the soil.'

The sapper went back to sifting through the dirt with his trowel. Cruikshank leaned against the wall of the well, his fist pressed to his mouth.

It was like a bad dream. His whole life had been an obsessive search for the contents of that vial. He didn't know why and never had. And now those contents were gone.

He felt a jab in his leg and looked down.

He was leaning against one of the thorn bushes. The hairs rose on Cruikshank's neck, as he realized what the sapper had been saying.

—Whatever was in the vial has leaked away into the soil.

—Bloody thorn bushes all over the shop. They cut me to ribbons.

237

Cruikshank slowly took a step away from the thorns and away from the sapper. He tapped his earpiece to make sure it was working.

The man was still crouching on the ground, but something about the shape of his shoulders had changed—as if he were tensing his muscles, ready to spring, like a cornered animal. He slowly turned his head, his eyes hidden by the shadow of his helmet rim. He grinned, a huge smile that glowed in Cruikshank's flashlight beam. He looked as if he had too many teeth.

'You came back for me after all,' he said.

The sapper's voice sounded very different from a few seconds ago. It was the voice the colonel had heard coming from May-Rose twenty years before. He remembered what she had said as if it were yesterday.

—*YOU COME BACK! COME BACK AND SAVE ME!*

And suddenly Cruikshank understood.

He understood why he had been driven to make a time machine. Understood his lifelong obsession with recovering May-Rose's genetic material. He had done it all because he could not disobey that terrible command.

Cruikshank had done exactly what the voice had told him to. He had gone back. He had saved whatever May-Rose had become.

And now he was free.

'This is Colonel Cruikshank,' he bellowed into his headset mike. 'A plague virus is loose in the bottom of the well! Evacuate and blanket bomb this whole area!'

The sapper scuttled sideways and grabbed hold of the pick.

'DON'T YOU MO—' he began, but the colonel lashed out with his boot. The kick caught the sapper in the throat and he fell backwards with a furious screech.

'Sir?' His second-in-command sounded both terrified and disbelieving. 'We can't do . . .'

'That's a code red order!' Cruikshank screamed, pulling his sidearm from its holster. The sapper lunged forwards, swinging the pick with all his might.

As the blade embedded itself in Cruikshank's chest, the colonel discharged his pistol into the bag of blasting caps.

Cruikshank's second-in-command threw himself to the ground as the earth shook and a ball of flame blossomed out of the well. He got to his feet and ran to the edge of the shaft, dodging clods of falling earth, but he knew nobody could have survived down there. He stopped at the blackened rim and peered into the darkness.

The colonel's last words had been a direct order—blanket bomb the area—an order that would mean the destruction of a multi-million pound research facility. It was an impossible directive.

But his second-in-command had heard rumours about why the original base had been destroyed. Whispers that had something to do with an outbreak of plague.

He clapped a hand over his mouth and retreated

from the edge, holding his breath. He had never really liked his superior but he knew one thing for certain.

Colonel Cruikshank was no fool.

The second-in-command tapped a button on his own handcom. The Communications Officer appeared on the screen.

'Start evacuating the base and then get me Headquarters,' he said. 'I think we have a real problem.'

At 8 o'clock in the evening, on Tuesday, 24 December 2027, Pinegrove Military Installation was destroyed by a series of massive explosions. The blast ripped apart acres of forest and devastated the remote highland valley where the base was located.

No official cause was given for the incident.

EPILOGUE: 2048

It was Christmas Day.

Madrid stood in the doorway of the ranger station, looking out across the forest. The building was a ruin now and the woodland was different too. The original trees were gone, cut down, she supposed. In its place, saplings of Douglas fir had been planted in neat orderly rows, like troops lined up for battle. The new woods must have been here for some time, however, for they had grown to near maturity.

Earlier that day she had walked through the forest to where Pinegrove had once stood, but the military base was completely gone. There weren't even any ruins, only more rows of trees. They looked somehow sinister—darker and thicker than other parts of the woodland and she had left quickly.

A cooing started up from the broken masonry behind her. On the crooked remnants of the chimney stack two pigeons ruffled their feathers and nestled up to each other.

She turned back and gave a start.

A man was walking through the trees towards her.

He was dressed in a dark top, jeans, and boots and wore a heavy black leather jacket. In one hand he carried a package wrapped in blue Christmas paper. As he got closer she studied his face.

241

Jimmy Hicks hadn't grown much taller; she judged that he was still a couple of inches shorter than she was. His floppy hair was cut short and going grey at the sides. He had filled out, his shoulders and chest were broad, and he no longer stooped when he walked.

He had turned into a handsome man, Madrid thought, though she could see that he had a large scar running down the side of his face. Madrid wondered how he got it. She wondered if he was married or had children. She realized with a shock that he looked a bit like Sherman.

Jimmy closed the gap between them, puffs of condensation scooting from his mouth. He stopped a few feet away.

'We finally get our date, Hicks,' Madrid said casually.

'Yeah. Sorry I'm late.' Jimmy moved forward until he was standing in front of her.

Madrid looked around the forest. She glanced up at the sky, then down to the ground. The man in front of her stayed motionless, waiting. Madrid put her hands behind her back and shuffled her feet. Finally, she tilted her head and tentatively glanced at Jimmy Hicks through long, thick lashes.

He gave a small smile.

'Ah. *There* you are, Lesley.'

Leaning forward he kissed the woman gently on her lips.

And they held each other for a long, long time.

Jan-Andrew Henderson was born in Dundee in 1962. After graduating he travelled for several years—but wherever he went, he wrote and staged plays, in places as far apart as the Edinburgh Festival and Texas. In 1998, he settled in Scotland and set up Black Hart Entertainment, one of the largest ghost tour companies in the UK. A year later he began writing non-fiction, bringing out *The Town Below the Ground*, *The Emperor's New Kilt*, *The Ghost that Haunted Itself*, *The Wee Book of Edinburgh*, *Who Wants to be an Edinburgher?*, and *City of the Dead*. After the birth of his son, he moved on to writing children's fiction. *Bunker 10* is his first novel for older readers, and his third for Oxford University Press.